Romance Unbound Publishing

The Master & the Secretary

Claire Thompson

Edited by Jae Ashley

Fine line edit by Gabriella Wolek

Cover Art by Mayhem Cover Creations

Previously titled: Confessions of a Submissive – completely updated, revised & enhanced

ISBN 978-1980520207
Copyright 2018 Claire Thompson

All rights reserved

Chapter 1

"What's this?"

Tess pushed aside the pile of old newspapers and photo albums to reveal a small strongbox. She pulled it free and set it down on a bare spot in the cluttered attic. The clasp was secured with a small but sturdy padlock. She pulled at it, but it didn't give.

The landline ringing downstairs distracted her, and Tess rushed down to answer it. "Winston residence," she said, slightly out of breath.

"Olivia." The voice was deep and resonant.

"Excuse me, who's calling?"

There was a slight pause. "Forgive me, I thought you were Olivia. Is she available, please?"

"Oh, um…" Tess hesitated. "Who is this, please?"

Another pause. "This is James Stevenson. I'm-I'm a good friend of Olivia's. I've been out of the country for the past month. I'm afraid I'm no good with all this internet and cell phone stuff, and I've been out of touch. Is Olivia all right?"

Tess could hear the sudden concern in the man's voice, and she steeled herself for what she had to say. "I hate to be the bearer of bad news, but my grandmother passed away three weeks ago. It was very sudden." Tears sprang to Tess's eyes as she shared the sad news.

"No," the man said in a sharp exhale of breath, as if he'd just been punched in the solar plexus. "That can't be right. I saw her right before I left and she was perfectly fine. She can't be gone." His voice cracked. "I-I-I..." He trailed off, and Tess wondered if the poor man was crying.

"I'm so sorry," Tess said gently. "She passed away very peacefully in her sleep. Her heart just gave out. The funeral was last week."

"I see," he said slowly, sounding as if he were struggling beneath a ten-ton weight. "Thank you for...for letting me know."

Tess heard the click of his receiver and she gently cradled her own.

James Stevenson. *A good friend,* he had said, and clearly one who was devastated by the news of her passing. She tried to recall Nana's ever having mentioned him, but came up with nothing. Who was this mysterious James Stevenson?

Tess's eyes filled with tears for the hundredth time that weekend as her gaze fell on a photograph of Nana and Pop. It was from early in their marriage, sometime in the fifties. Nana was smiling, the big happy smile of someone young and in love. Her face was turned toward her husband, who stared directly ahead, his expression self-conscious and stiff as he posed for the lens.

Olivia's hair was pulled back in a careless ponytail, tendrils of unruly hair against her cheeks. Her face looked fresh and open. A Kansas farm girl kind of freshness, with a sprinkling of freckles across her broad, snubbed nose.

Tess held the framed photo, one she'd looked at many times before, and mentally compared herself with the woman she saw there. In the old picture, Nana was younger even than Tess's twenty-five years. Where Olivia had been strawberry blond and blue-eyed, Tess had her father's dark brown hair and brooding brown eyes. She had always envied her Nana's open, sunny countenance.

Next to the photo were several large seashells, their horny exteriors protecting the delicate, milky pink curves inside. Tess lifted a nautilus shell, cradling it gently in her hands. It brought back sharp memories of summers spent collecting shells at dawn, while everyone but she and Nana slept. The world had seemed to belong only to the two of them then.

Tess sighed loudly and wiped a tear from her cheek with the back of her hand. Everything about this old house was steeped in memories of Nana and Pop. She thought about the box she'd discovered in the attic. What was in there that had to be kept locked?

Tess recalled a ring of keys in Nana's desk when she was going through old papers. Hurrying over to the desk, she pulled open the drawers, rooting around until she found the keys behind a container of pushpins and paper clips. Examining it, she noted a small key that might fit the padlock.

Returning to the attic, she knelt in front of the strongbox and fit the key into the lock, her heart beating with anticipation.

It wouldn't budge.

Frustrated, she tried all the other keys, but none were even close. It was getting late, and she had several hours of work to do to get ready for an important meeting the next day. The strongbox would have to wait.

Tess returned the next evening to her grandmother's house, the locked strongbox still on her mind. Who knew what was in it? Maybe precious jewels and gold coins—that was what Nana would have said, rubbing her hands together in gleeful anticipation of the discovery. Maybe it contained love letters from Nana's first boyfriend or something. More likely, it contained those old S&H green stamps booklets Nana had loved to collect in the sixties when she was a young housewife and mother, eagerly saving for a new blender or sewing machine.

Before entering the house, Tess went into the shed in the backyard, where she retrieved a bolt cutter, just in case her continued search for a key didn't yield results. In the house, she looked through all the drawers, especially the night table on Nana's side of the bed, but no luck.

She climbed the attic stairs, bolt cutter in hand, as she tried to think where Nana might have hidden that key. All at once, Tess remembered the long summers at Nana and Pop's summer beach cottage. "The key's on the window ledge, dear," she could almost hear Nana say. "If we're down at the shore when you get here, just let yourself in."

There were two windows in the attic, one on either side. Tess went over to one of them and felt along the top of the window, finding nothing but dust and bits of chipped paint. Crossing the room, she ran her fingers along the second ledge. Something scuttled away from her fingers, causing her to jerk her hand away and let out an involuntary squeal.

Recovering herself, she put her hand again up to the dusty ledge and slowly moved her fingers along it until they bumped against something flat and cold to the touch. She closed her fingers around a small key with a satisfied smile. Nana would have been proud of her detective work.

Quickly she walked over to the strongbox, for the first time considering if she had the right to open it. She wavered for a second, debating if she should ask her mother's opinion. But her curiosity won out. It wasn't like she would do anything to compromise Nana's privacy.

Putting any misgivings to rest, she pushed the key into the lock. It turned smoothly with a satisfying click, and slowly she opened the lid.

No jewelry, no S&H green stamps. There were just some old notebooks. They were thin, with pale blue covers, like composition booklets for a final exam. Old account ledgers? Tess lifted the top one, which had the number five written in the upper right hand corner. The other notebooks were numbered as well, one through four.

Selecting what she assumed was the first in the series, she opened it and immediately recognized her grandmother's neat, flowing handwriting. Wildly curious, Tess began to read.

~*~

October 11, 1961

Mr. Stevenson said I should write in this journal. He said it would help me to sort out my thoughts. He told me to get myself a little notebook and keep it here at work somewhere safe.

I'm not sure where to start.

When I asked Mr. Stevenson where he thought I should, he said, in that deep voice of his, "Start at the beginning. And be honest. Explore your feelings and don't censor yourself. No one but you will read your private thoughts."

"Not even you?" I asked him.

"Most especially not me."

I believe him. I think it would go against his grain to lie.

Well, I shall start at the beginning, as Mr. Stevenson instructed.

Mr. James Stevenson is an attorney, and I am his secretary. I can't believe Frank let me go back to work, but since Jeannie is in second grade already, and I'm so bored at home, he said it was all right. Plus, I know the extra money will help with our summer vacations. I've already saved up some since I started here in early September.

~*~

James Stevenson, the man who had called the other day. The good friend... Tess was aware Nana had worked in an attorney's office when she was young. Whatever had developed between them had to be more than just secretary and boss, as evidenced by the fact they were still in touch fifty years later, and Mr. Stevenson characterized himself as a good friend.

Tess was confused, and not a little intrigued. Why in the world would Nana's boss instruct her to keep a journal? It was time to read on and find out.

~*~

October 12, 1961

Mr. Stevenson is a very exacting man, and he insists on perfection. He reminds me time and again that an attorney can't afford to make mistakes, and therefore neither can his secretary. The first time he whacked my hand with the ruler, I have to admit I was surprised, but I'm coming to see that it is indeed effective. My typing has improved markedly.

~*~

What the hell was this? Tess looked at it again to make sure she hadn't misread. Whacking her hand with a ruler? This was no ordinary office situation, even if it was way back in 1961.

Tess shifted on the hard attic floor. Getting to her feet, she scooped up the pile of notebooks and went downstairs. She made herself a cup of tea, prolonging the moment when she returned to the bizarre journal.

For the first time, her comfortable, confident knowledge of who and what her grandmother had been was shaken. She considered for a moment tossing the notebooks unread and forgetting she had ever seen them. But even as she thought this, she dismissed it. There was no way she was going to throw these out. She was going to read these things from beginning to end. She had to know.

Sitting down at Nana's old Formica table, Tess sipped her cinnamon tea and lifted the first journal again.

~*~

October 13, 1961

I can't believe he used the ruler on my bottom yesterday! Especially just for a silly thing like a run in my stocking. I can't even believe I'm sitting here writing this, but Mr. Stevenson has given me an extra-long lunch hour, and he told me to use it wisely. I know he wants me to write. Probably afraid if I don't get it out here, I'll tell Frank my employer smacked my rear with a ruler!

How did all this happen? When did my boss become this bizarre disciplinarian? At first, he seemed like your normal everyday old boss. Well, maybe not "everyday," as he's always been a stickler for perfection, right from the beginning.

Distinguished-looking and very much the proper attorney. He's thirty-four, I know because I saw his birth date on some of his certification records. He's married and has two sons. His last secretary was named Millicent Willis. She quit this past year when she married, and so he needed someone new.

Thinking back, the interview *was* rather unusual, but I was so eager for the job that I brushed it aside. I remember now how he went on and on about how exacting he was, and how he'd grown used to Miss Willis' 120 word-per-minute dictation. I don't believe that—I do 105 and I'm very fast. I remember he went on about her ability to proof a legal document and catch every single teeny-tiny error. He said if he hired me, I'd be on probation for six weeks and that I'd be punished for any infraction.

Yes! He actually said punished, and when I raised my eyebrows and said, "Excuse me?" he kind of backtracked, explaining that he only meant he was very exacting and wouldn't tolerate incompetence. In short, I'd either be up to his high standards or out the door.

But I'm coming to realize you can't be up to Mr. Stevenson's standards. They're impossible. I'd really like to meet this Miss Willis. She must be a saint here on this earth, with her perfect skills and perfect everything else. Makes me want to slap her!

What is it about Mr. Stevenson that makes me want to please him so?

Partly, it's that voice. Sonorous. That's the word that comes to mind. It's pleasing, but more than that, it's commanding. Lulling, lilting, moving. I feel like I'm tethered to him on some secret level and his voice draws me to him. One wants to immediately obey whatever he asks. One wants, almost desperately, to please.

His voice haunts me. I dream of it. But the things he expects? And these bizarre little punishments. Why do I tolerate the smack of his ruler and his relentless critiquing of my apparently numerous failings?

What in God's name is wrong with me?

October 17, 1961

Yesterday, I told Mr. Stevenson that I quit. He said he wouldn't accept the resignation. I said, "Why ever not? I obviously don't measure up to Miss Magnificent Willis."

"Come into my office, Olivia," he said, not even looking back to see if I followed. Well, I did follow, waiting to see what he had to say. Frank has already come to rely on my paycheck, and I dreaded telling him I'd quit, but enough is enough.

What precipitated my decision? Well, yesterday morning Mr. Stevenson told me two very important clients were coming in and he wanted to make sure we made an excellent impression, as they could throw a lot more business our way. He actually asked me to bend over so he could inspect the back of my stockings. Given that run last week, he explained, as if it were perfectly natural for a boss to inspect his secretary's legs!

That's part of it—the way he's so confident and sure when he's "disciplining" me. The way he acts as if this were the most natural thing in the world between a boss and his secretary. I find myself blushing and stammering, desperate to please him, chagrined, humiliated even, when I have failed yet again to measure up.

I find myself saying, "I'm sorry, sir, it won't happen again." And while it's happening, it doesn't occur to me that this is very odd behavior on both our parts. I haven't worked in a law office before, it's true, but I'm certain most attorneys don't keep a ruler at the ready to smack their errant secretaries. And probably most girls would have been out the door after the first rap to their knuckles.

Yet here I sit, writing in this thing because he told me to and instead of protesting, I try harder and harder to please Mr. Stevenson. I don't know why exactly. There's something about him. I haven't conveyed it at all here. I haven't really conveyed much of anything yet, I guess, except that I must be stone-cold crazy.

Suffice it to say, there's something about Mr. Stevenson. You just want to please him. Yet, it's so hard to do. So, when you do succeed in getting that little half-smile of approval, you feel so good and proud.

Yesterday morning when he instructed me to bend over, for some absurd reason I actually complied, bending over the back of my chair with no idea what might come next. Well, he actually lifted the skirt, right up to my derrière, and then he ran his hands slowly up and down my thighs, as if he had every right.

"Mr. Stevenson!" I admonished in a shocked tone, standing up at once as I pushed his hands away.

I know, I know. Before that, I had let this man swat my hand and my leg and even my bottom (over my skirt) with his little ruler, and here I was acting all affronted. Why didn't I quit before? I can't say exactly. But yesterday was the last straw.

I fumed over it all through my lunch hour, which I took at my desk because it was raining and I didn't want to sit in the park like I usually do. He left, as usual, promptly at one o'clock and returned on the dot of two.

God, listen to me, writing to myself and lying! I'm lying to myself right here on this page, as if I were a stranger who is going to read this and judge me. What is wrong with me?

It wasn't that I was so upset by his feeling my thigh.

It was that I was so aroused by it!

There. I've said it.

Frank would never touch me like that—not in a million years. Frank is, well, Frank. Boring Frank. Make love to your wife once a week on Fridays, and keep your eyes closed, no doubt thinking about your next fishing trip, and moving just enough to finish before Jack Parr comes on the television.

God. I can't believe I wrote that. I love Frank! I do. But sex. It's so boring. I've read that it can be wonderful, that it can send tingles through you. You know, I'm just realizing as I sit here writing this that that's exactly it. Mr. Stevenson's hand sent tingles through me, right to that hot spot in my center. I wanted him to keep touching me, to move higher.

It was me I was mad at, not him.

Because I'm married, for better or for worse, so what the hell am I doing? Mr. Stevenson made me think, just for a second, mind you, of someone else. In our eleven years of marriage, I've never so much as looked at another man, and now my boss, of all people, is becoming the center of my fantasies.

Well, I had just finished typing my resignation, feeling very proper and formal. And very nervous. I pulled it out of my typewriter and handed it to him as he passed, saying, "I'm sorry, Mr. Stevenson, but you really give me no choice."

That's when he told me to come into his office. "Sit down, please, Olivia." He looked me up and down in that slow deliberate way he has, like the headmaster at an old-fashioned boarding school in England. I almost expected him to sigh and say that now he would have no choice but to call my parents.

In fact, he said, "I think your decision is hasty. Let's discuss it."

Well, I sat and I crossed my legs and folded my arms across my chest, my chin held high. There was no way he was going to change my mind. Then he totally shocked me.

"Olivia, I want you to know you are no longer on probation. The overall quality of your work is excellent, but that isn't why I want to keep you on. There's something else. I think you know what I'm talking about."

"No, sir, I don't," I snapped. I was being snooty, but frankly, it felt good, because I kept telling myself that after today I wasn't going to have to come in there anymore and be treated like some kind of wayward child. At the same time, I found myself thrilling to his rare words of praise. Excellent work quality! But that "something else"—I pretended to him, and for a split second, to myself, that I had no earthly idea what he meant.

I was lying.

I can admit it here, because nobody but me will ever see this.

This is my secret.

I *did* know what he meant. I don't mean I could articulate it. I'm still not sure I can, but there's something. God, it's embarrassing even to write it here, where no one can see it, but I did know what he meant.

When Mr. Stevenson checks my work my heart starts pounding, and I wait on tenterhooks to see what he'll do. Always that ruler, tap, tap, tapping against his thigh while he reads, carefully, looking—hoping?—for an error, a mistake, something out of place, something missing, so he can say, his voice serious, "Olivia, you've made an error. Come here, and I'll show you." Carefully he points it out, that perfectly manicured fingernail glinting against the misspelled word or an incorrect usage. Calmly, he'll say, "Olivia, hold out your hand."

Thwack!

Oh, it smarts when he hits my hand. I've tried it different ways, palm up, palm down. I think palm up is easier to take, but he must know this too because he'll hit me harder when I offer my palm.

Okay, I'm getting to it. I'm just going to write this and maybe it will help me understand. Mr. Stevenson says sometimes you know a thing, even when you don't know you know it. What he meant, and what I understood but couldn't express, was that I *liked* what he did to me.

There, I wrote it here, and now I'm blushing, even though I'm sitting here all alone. It isn't just his hand on my thigh or that lovely compelling voice or his good looks. It's everything. The ruler, the stern expression, the exacting requirements that always keep me on my toes.

Mr. Stevenson went to lunch on the stroke of one, just like always. He goes home to lunch with Mrs. Stevenson, I suppose. I've never asked. I would never ask about his personal life and he never asks about mine.

And I'm still sitting here.

"You need discipline, Olivia," he said, smiling a little. "I sensed that in you the moment we met. You've never been disciplined because you're smart and you're used to getting away with things because of that. But I can see through it. I know who you are—I know what you are. And I'm going to teach you to understand. Little by little, but trust me, you will learn. I've been very careful with you up until now, testing the waters, you might say.

"But you've forced my hand with this absurd resignation letter." As he spoke, he tore it up. He actually tore it up into tiny pieces, letting them flutter to the ground. "I won't let you go." He stared at me for a moment, his stern expression softening. In an almost gentle tone, he said, "I need you, Olivia. Forgive my presumption, but you need me too. You need what I offer you."

I stared back at him, not giving him a lick of help. But inside, my brain was in a jumble, my gut in a clench. I *did* need what he offered, whatever the hell it was he was offering.

Then he took my breath with his next remark. "You, Olivia, are going to become my submissive. You will belong to me so completely you will never again even contemplate the thought of leaving me. Ever. Do you understand?"

He actually said that. All of it. I remember what people say. Mr. Stevenson says it's a useful quality, as I can recall exact words that were spoken when he has me sit in on some of his meetings, even without consulting my notes.

Submissive.

I looked it up later. It isn't even a noun, but he uses it as if it were. *To submit,* "To yield oneself to the authority or will of another. To surrender. To permit oneself to be subjected to something."

"I have come to value you," he went on and then he told me he was giving me a twenty percent raise, right there on the spot, effective immediately. He said he wasn't trying to buy me off, but that he wanted to demonstrate in some tangible way how much he valued me.

Well, I pretended that that was what swayed me and I don't mind saying that Frank will be pretty happy about it. But in truth, it wasn't the money. It was the way he said he valued me. The sincerity in his voice and how handsome he looked as he said it. And the way he tore up the letter, like some movie with Gregory Peck—he even looks a little like Gregory Peck. It was very dramatic.

Okay, okay, I'm not being totally honest. As usual. It was also the ruler and all that it implies. I like the ruler—the discipline and the thinly veiled sexual overtones. It makes me aroused. And the way he talked about me belonging to him. I'm not even sure what all he meant, but I got a deep little thrill, right down to my toes, when he said it.

I can't believe I'm writing this. I must be crazy.

Chapter 2

"Oh my god," Tess breathed, stunned at what she'd been reading. She set down the diary and gazed absently at the sampler Nana had cross-stitched that had hung over the sink in Nana's kitchen for as long as Tess could remember—"Blessed Are Those Who Clean Up." Now that was the Nana Tess knew. Funny, homey, down-to-earth. Not a sexual bone in her body. Who the hell was this other woman, this secretary who had a boss with a ruler? A handsome Gregory Peck boss with very "exacting" standards.

And it had happened way back in 1961. People didn't do stuff like that back then, did they? There was no internet, no postings on personals sites—*Stern boss seeks submissive secretary. Must take dictation and spankings.*

And yet... And yet, if Tess were honest, as honest as her grandmother was in her diary, were the feelings expressed there really so foreign? Tess, like her grandmother, had as yet unexplored submissive feelings of her own. Her secret fantasies of being held down and "taken" by her lover had remained just that—secret. But they were there.

The idea of working for some guy who was into control... While Tess rejected the idea on the surface, her body was responding otherwise. As bizarre as it was, what she was reading turned her on, even if it was her old Nana who had written the words.

Again she marveled, shaking her head. Her grandmother having submissive thoughts and feelings, all those years ago. It didn't seem possible. Yet, here were these journals, written in Nana's neat, precise hand, the blue ink faded on paper yellowed with time.

This Mr. Stevenson... Tess had half a mind to call him back and demand an explanation. And yet, she was the one reading someone else's most secret thoughts and dreams. This wasn't any of Tess's business. She thought of herself as free and liberated, sexually and otherwise. Why should she expect a different set of behaviors for her grandmother, just because she was older and of another generation?

Don't judge her, Tess warned herself. That was something Nana had often said. "Don't judge someone just because they don't think exactly like you do. Until you've walked in their shoes, you just have no idea." Well, she was obviously speaking from experience, wasn't she?

Tea forgotten, Tess picked up the journal and continued to read.

~*~

October 19, 1961

Frank was tickled pink about the raise. He's never admitted it, but he didn't think I had what it took to be a secretary. He use to say the secretarial school I attended after high school was just a front while I went after my "MRS" degree. He never thought I was cut out for much more than changing diapers and making cookies. But money talks, as Frank is fond of saying, and money is telling him now I'm worth something.

Since we had that little talk, Mr. Stevenson has said straight out he's going to "train" me to behave in a way proper to my station—he actually used those words. The man is something out of a Dickens' novel.

Things have been moving pretty fast. Maybe a little too fast for me.

Yesterday, when I brought in his coffee, I spilled a little when I set it down. The saucer slipped and the coffee slopped over the edge so that a little got on his precious walnut desktop. I had to go back to the kitchenette to get a dishtowel, and when I returned, he was standing behind his chair, holding that ruler. I felt a twinge in my belly.

"Olivia," he intoned. "Have you any idea what this desk is worth? It's been in my family for generations. I can't have it being ruined by some careless secretary, now can I?"

"No, sir," I whispered, my breath catching in my throat. He looked so handsome, so stern, standing there, tapping the ruler against the top of his chair.

"You've been here long enough to know the rules. But perhaps they need to be spelled out more clearly for you, since you continue to behave in such a cavalier fashion when it comes to precious antiques."

It was just a drop of coffee, not some federal offense, for heaven's sake. I actually blurted that out to him, and his whole countenance darkened.

"First rule, Olivia, is that you don't offer your opinions, unless I ask for them. I am the boss here. You are not. Is that understood?"

"Yes, sir," I said, looking down as heat seared my cheeks. This was crazy. I knew it, and yet it wasn't crazy either. Something about it felt so right—so exciting.

Again the tap, tap, tap of that ruler. "Second rule. From now on, first infraction is ten strokes with the ruler. Either on your knuckles or on your bottom. I should warn you that I won't be using it so lightly anymore. Now that you're in formal training, your punishments will be real. Repeated infractions will receive escalated punishment. Do I make myself clear?"

"Um..." I hesitated.

"Speak plainly, Olivia. Do not say 'um.' You are not a schoolgirl. Do I make myself clear?"

I swallowed. "Well, Mr. Stevenson, not entirely. I mean, are you saying that you plan to, um, use that ruler on my *bottom*?" I blushed saying this out loud. But he had said it first. I kept going since he just looked at me, his arms folded over that nice broad chest of his. "Is that over the skirt? Is this legal? And if you hit my hand too hard, what if it marks me somehow? My husband might wonder."

"Your husband is not my concern, Olivia. How you handle yourself at home is entirely your affair. While you are here at the office, you belong to me. If you are concerned that some easily visible possible bruising or mark might be questioned, I would suggest you avail yourself of the second method, that is, your bottom. And yes, first infraction will be over the skirt. After that, we shall see. As to legalities, you and I have not entered into any sort of legal contract. I consider what happens here between us to be on both a professional and personal level. That is, I expect you to behave professionally at all times, but our arrangement, by its nature, is personal. Legality doesn't enter into it."

He stood there for a moment, waiting. Maybe he expected me to tell him to go to hell. Maybe he was waiting to see if I would run out of there screaming.

I didn't do either.

I just stood there staring at him like a tongue-tied idiot. Inside I was almost sick with the adrenaline rush I was feeling. My gut was churning like I was on a roller coaster and I felt giddy with anticipation, though not really sure of what. I suppose he took my silence for acquiescence, and I guess it was.

He went on, with a slight nod, as if I had spoken, as if I had given him permission. "Now, you have spilled coffee on my desk. That is infraction number one. Then you protested and argued that it was 'just a drop coffee,' which clearly indicates to me that you don't value my property in a way that befits your station. That is infraction number two. I shall teach you the value of my things."

He cleared his throat. "At the end of each day we shall tally your infractions, and I will decide upon a punishment. You will accept the punishment with grace. Failure to comply immediately with my dictate will incur another infraction. Am I clear, Olivia?"

My mouth felt dry. Part of me was furious with this arrogant man. How *dare* he talk to me like I was some kind of servant or slave from medieval times, and he the lord and master of the realm! But most of me was thunderstruck. Yes, that's the word. It's like he was speaking some secret language to me. Some language I didn't know I understood. Something that bypassed my brain and went right to my nerve endings.

I responded in that secret language, I guess. Some kind of weird sense of peace seemed to fall over me as I bowed my head and answered, "Yes, sir. You are clear, sir. I apologize about the coffee. I'll be more careful."

"Good," he nodded, looking pleased. "Now get your pad and take a letter. Punishment will be at 4:00 p.m. Sharp."

~*~

A secret language. Tess sat still, staring at the neat writing, the ink pale and fine as insect legs on the page. It was as if she were there in the room with Mr. Stevenson, taking Olivia's place, as thunderstruck— and as thrilled—as her grandmother had been.

Tess had started reading these journals with a sort of superior skepticism. Her sweet, innocent Nana—young Livvie from another era— subjected to the strange perversions of an overstepping boss. At the very least, it was just another hackneyed affair between a man and his secretary.

Yet, Tess found herself getting caught up in the drama of what she was reading. This talk of secret languages and punishments. Her nipples tingled, her pussy gently throbbing, stirred by the words on the page. She squirmed in her chair, pressing her legs together as she read on.

~*~

October 23, 1961

I've been tempted to take this journal home. Sometimes I write entries in my head while I'm washing the dishes or doing laundry or whatever. Or later, when Frank and I are lying in bed, the kids finally asleep. I'll be reading my novel as usual, with Frank beside me watching TV, and I'll get this ridiculous urge to confide in him. To tell him about the crazy things that are happening at work, and get his opinion.

Can you imagine? Frank would divorce me on the spot, or have me locked in the loony bin. Then he'd go threaten Mr. Stevenson with his stupid hunting shotgun.

Of course, Mr. Stevenson's right. It would be stupid to leave this journal lying around at home. Beyond stupid. Dangerous. Sometimes I wonder if Mr. Stevenson knows what I'm writing in here. If he knows that I think he looks like Gregory Peck, and that I get all excited and squirmy when he smacks my bottom.

But he doesn't read it. At least he hasn't yet. Maybe I really do have the only key to my desk drawers. I know he hasn't read it so far because I've been doing like they do in those detective novels. I put a strand of my hair very carefully across the cover of the journal. You couldn't really see it unless you were looking for it. And it hasn't been moved. That makes me feel safer, I suppose. These words are just for me.

Well, Friday afternoon was amazing. I actually think Mr. Stevenson manufactured one of the infractions in order to increase my punishment. It was during dictation and I swear he said "confidant" but he said no, it was supposed to be "confidence." After lecturing me about being precise in legal documents, he said, "Infraction number three."

It was very hard to concentrate for the rest of the afternoon. I didn't do much of anything at all from three thirty to four o'clock, except check my face in my compact, reapply my lipstick and powder, adjust my stockings, go to the bathroom, fluff my hair. It was like I was going for an audition or on a blind date!

When four o'clock arrived, I sat on tenterhooks, waiting for his one-word command.

"Olivia."

I got to my feet, trying to keep my jangling nerves under control. The door was ajar so I walked in, feeling like I was heading into the principal's office after being caught with cigarettes.

He was sitting at his desk, his pen poised over some document, head bowed. The rat kept looking at his papers, like they were too important to stop reading, even though he was the one who had called me in. I told myself he was just doing that to make me feel more ill at ease—more nervous. More compliant.

Well, it worked! I stood there, trying not to shift and shuffle like a little kid.

Finally, he looked up, as if only suddenly aware that I had entered the room. He looked me slowly up and down. I blushed. I know I did, because I could feel the heat in my face and neck. I tried to stand still—to act calm and collected, like Audrey Hepburn in *Roman Holiday*. And Mr. Stevenson was every bit as handsome as Gregory Peck in that movie. So dashing!

I actually had a sudden fantasy of rushing over and kissing him, right on the mouth! Of course, I did no such thing. He'd probably have fired me on the spot. I do not believe my crush on Mr. Stevenson is returned. At least not in a schoolboy kind of a way, all gushy and nervous like me. No, he is far too calm and collected for that sort of behavior.

Mr. Stevenson is into control.

He stood up and walked over to the leather couch on the far wall from his desk. He sat down and took his ruler, that ever-present ruler, from the arm of the couch where he'd obviously placed it before, in anticipation of my punishment.

"Come here, Olivia. How many infractions today?"

Like he didn't know.

"Three, Sir," I answered, knowing he would count the confidence/confidant dispute.

(Why did I just capitalize Sir? I don't know, but somehow it just seems…right.)

"That's correct. I'm going to give you a choice of punishment. You can take thirty over the skirt or"—he paused, his eyes boring into mine—"ten underneath."

Sweat prickled under my arms and my nipples pressed hard against my bra. I pursed my lips, pretending to weigh my options, but I'd already decided. If we were going to play this game, I thought, then let's do it right.

I'll admit something here.

I wanted to feel his hand on my bottom. Not my bare bottom, mind you. I'm not ready for that.

Yet.

Oh my God, did I just write that?

The idea of those long, tapered fingers touching my body in such an intimate way, such a dangerous and forbidden way, gets me all hot and bothered.

Trying to sound calm, I responded, "Ten, under the skirt."

He actually raised his eyebrows, as if he were surprised by my choice, and a ghost of a smile hovered around his mouth. "Very well. Take off the skirt. It's too narrow to hike up."

And I did it.

Mrs. Old Married Woman unzipped her skirt and laid it carefully over a chair. I stood there in my girdle and underpants, feeling very self-conscious indeed.

Though I feel kind of sorry for his wife—look what he's doing behind her back—in a way knowing that he's married makes me more comfortable. He's obviously seen a woman in this state of undress many times before. Probably doesn't even think twice about it.

He looked me over with a frown while the heat crept up my cheeks as usual. "I don't like girdles. Why do slender women like you wear girdles?"

Well, I liked that he called me slender. But married or not, he obviously didn't know much about women's undergarments. "To hold up my stockings, of course," I snapped, and then bit my lip, worried I had sounded "impertinent."

He let it pass, answering, "There are much nicer ways to do that, Olivia. Next Monday on your lunch hour, you will go to Slone's Dress Shop in the village and pick up a package. It will be in my name at the counter. You will not wear a girdle again in my presence, once you have the garter belts that will be waiting for you. Understood?"

The man was buying me underwear!

Instead of slapping his face and quitting again, I nodded, but I was thinking, "Garter belts?" I was going to dress like a common whore for this man who was my boss. I knew I was going to do it and I'll admit here, the notion excited me.

He drew me back to the matter at hand. "Come here and bend over my lap."

I felt awkward and sort of ridiculous, a grown woman balancing over a man's knee in her girdle and stockings.

But I did it.

Thwack! He smacked me really hard. Much harder than the little taps I'd been getting up until then.

"Ouch," I yelled involuntarily.

"Come now. This is nothing. Take it like a true submissive, Olivia. Silently." Again he smacked me, and I managed not to yelp out loud, though I did kind of grunt. I mean, it stung, even through the rubbery fabric of the girdle and my panties. Imagine it on bare skin. He did it eight more times, covering my entire bottom.

Here's the really weird thing.

The secret thing.

Afterward, my panties were soaked.

I was so aroused by that paddling that I couldn't wait to get home to Frank. Lucky for me it was Friday, so I was pretty much assured of some sex.

When Frank made love to me, after I finally got the kids off to bed, I think I actually might have had an orgasm. I'm not exactly sure, but I think I did. Anyway, it felt really good, and when he pressed my sore bottom against the sheets, it just made me so hot. I'm sure Frank must have wondered what had gotten into me. He isn't crazy about a woman showing too much emotion during sex. "Isn't seemly", he'd say if pressed. Not that he'd talk about it, but after eleven years, I know that's what he thinks.

I wonder what it's like for Mr. Stevenson and his wife. Does she get punished too? Or would she divorce him if he tried this stuff with her? And where is this going with Mr. Stevenson? Are we having an affair?

What am I doing????

October 23, 1961 – later

I'm spending too much time writing in this thing, but Mr. Stevenson assures me it's not a waste of time, so here goes—entry number two of the day.

The garter belts are beautiful. Elegant satin, one in cream, one in black and one in pearl gray. The place was so upscale. Nothing I'd ever go into on my own. They actually keep the door locked and have to buzz you in, and there's no price tag on anything. I guess if you have to ask...

The saleslady was very posh and sophisticated, and she acted like I was the Queen of England as she handed me the beautiful box wrapped with a pretty ribbon. When I got back to the office, Mr. Stevenson told me to open the package and select a belt. He says I'm to leave them at the office each evening, and put one on each morning when I arrive. He said I could wash them out here as necessary.

I'm wearing the pearl gray garter belt with my stockings. It really does feel better than a girdle, though it doesn't control my figure as well. I feel almost naked under there. I've been wearing a girdle for so long. I mean, everyone does. Still, I have to admit, it feels really sexy. Right now, as I'm writing, I'm fingering one of the satin ribbons at the bottom of the garter.

I can't wait for him to call me in to show him!

It's 4:15 and I have to leave in fifteen minutes so I'm home in time to cook dinner for Frank and the kids, but I have to get this out first.

I'm so annoyed. And confused!

I've been waiting all day, but nothing. Zilch. When he called me in for dictation, I thought, this is it, he'll ask me to raise my skirt and show him. The whole time he was dictating, I could barely keep my mind on what he was saying. Finally, he said, "Thank you, that will be all."

I just sat there, dumbfounded.

He cocked an eyebrow. "Was there something else, Olivia?"

I had to bite my tongue, let me tell you. Mr. Stevenson has yet to experience my sarcastic side. I lost my nerve though, muttering, "No, Sir. I'll get these typed up."

The whole rest of the afternoon went like that. When 4:00 came, I thought, well, this is it. Finally. Now he'll call me in to show him the sexy garters.

Well, 4:00 came and went, and nothing happened. Just now Mr. Stevenson came out of his office, barely stopping as he said, calm as you please, "Good night, Olivia."

That's it! Just good night. He took his overcoat and his hat, and, after reminding me to lock up, left.

Now I'm sitting here, just fuming! Is the man made of flesh and blood, or stone and metal? Aren't I an attractive woman?

I just reread what I wrote, and I think I'm losing my mind. Here I am, furious, because I've been waiting around all afternoon like an idiot for my boss to call me in and demand to see the garter belts he paid for. There is definitely something wrong with me. I wonder if I should see a doctor.

Chapter 3

October 25, 1961

Hope springs eternal, right? Surely if he hadn't asked to see the garters on Monday, he would on Tuesday. I managed to arrive early enough to put on my satin undies and sexy garter belt before Mr. Stevenson arrived. I chose the black set, with the pair of sheer black stockings I usually only wear when Frank and I go out somewhere fancy. Whether or not he was going to look at them, I was going to wear them. If I had anything to do with it, I was going to get that man to look at them.

When Mr. Stevenson came in, after a brusque good morning, he said, "I need the Masterson file right away. And a cup of coffee, if you please." Now, normally, I would have jumped up and gotten that file and brought it to him right away. Then off to the kitchenette to pour him a cup of coffee, prepared just the way he likes it, one sugar and plenty of cream. But not too much cream, or the coffee won't be hot enough.

Well, I didn't do either thing. I pretended to make a phone call, actually calling First Fidelity for that recording of time and temperature. Then I buffed a nail and reapplied my lipstick. Then I meandered to the kitchenette and made his coffee, but darn if I didn't add too much cream, whoops. Then, and only then, I got the file he wanted, but oh dear, it was the Masters file, instead of the Masterson.

I chickened out when it actually came to spilling the coffee. That would have been overkill, and God knows I don't want to be the one responsible for destroying his family heirloom. I set the cup and saucer on his desk alongside the incorrect file.

He didn't look up or act as if he knew I existed.

I went back to my desk.

After a while, he came out and got the proper file himself, dumping the wrong one onto my desk without looking at me. But still he hadn't said a word.

Damn him, the morning went on as any other. I kept waiting for him to call me in, but not a word. I was too nervous to eat my lunch. Here I'd gone and messed things up on purpose, just to see what he would do, and he didn't do a thing.

But then, at 4:00 on the nose he intoned, "Olivia."

Finally!

I got up and went into his office, after a quick check of my makeup. I knew I'd earned a punishment, and I was both terrified and thrilled.

Things didn't go precisely as I'd planned them. To put it mildly.

I'm not even exactly sure what happened, but I figure if I write it down here, it will help me sort it out.

When I entered the office, Mr. Stevenson said, "Close the door." He had never said that before, since we're the only two in the office, but I obeyed, my heart pounding a mile a minute.

He just stood there behind his chair for a while, looking me up and down. "The mouse," he finally said, "is toying with the cat. The mouse," he went on, "likes to play, and sees this all as a little game. The mouse"— now he stared at me until I blushed and looked down—"will have to learn this is no game."

Well, I was squirming like a kid again and wishing I could start the day over. What had I been thinking? Sophisticated Mr. Stevenson wasn't going to fall for my obvious little ploys.

"You need to be punished. That much is clear. Not because you brought me the wrong file, but because you did it on purpose. Not because my coffee had too much cream, but because you did that on purpose as well.

"You are toying with me, and I must say, your manipulations lack subtlety." I blushed at this, let me tell you, but he wasn't done. "Some clarification apparently needs to be made. You need to be taught that it is I, not you, who initiates punishments, who decides what is and what is not an infraction, and who determines how you will behave when you are here. Go to the corner."

"What?"

"Go to the corner, and put your nose against the wall. Women who act like naughty little girls will be treated as such. You willfully tried to manipulate me into using a ruler on you, like a kid trying to trick her daddy into buying her candy. So, go on, little girl. Nose against the wall. Hands behind your back. Grab each elbow with the opposite hand and stand perfectly still. Go on. Do it, or get out."

Well, I had no intention of obeying such a ridiculous order. You can bet I wasn't going to. But something in his tone compelled me to obey. My legs felt like rubber, but somehow I got myself over to the corner. In an almost trancelike state, I leaned over and touched my nose to the wall. He made me stand out farther from the wall, so that I had to stick out my rear to keep my nose in place.

I was mortified. That's the best word for it. Mortified and humiliated.

And on fire.

I felt so ridiculous with my nose pressed against the wall, holding my hands behind my back. But that tingle was there too. I realized I was waiting for him to come up behind me. To press slowly against me, like in the movies, and maybe let my bun down or something. I don't know what exactly I was expecting.

Stop lying, Livvie. You know exactly what you were expecting, or even hoping, would happen.

I fantasized right there on the spot that he would lean over me and kiss my neck, and maybe whisper something sexy about me belonging to him. My ears were pricked, waiting to hear him approach. I was so excited, even though I felt so silly with my face in the corner. Something was about to happen. He could say what he liked about manipulation, but here I was, waiting for the exciting, sexy, dangerous thing to happen—the thing I'd willed into being by my actions.

Well, it didn't. Nothing. Zippo. Just me standing there, my nose against the wall, feeling more and more ridiculous. After a while, I got a crick in my neck. My arms started to ache as I tried to balance with my nose while holding my elbows behind me. All the while, he just stood there, or whatever he was doing. For all I knew, he had left the room. I didn't dare turn around to find out.

I stayed in the corner for three hours. No, it couldn't have been, but it felt like it. Finally, he spoke from behind me, the sound of his voice making me startle. "Good night, Olivia. I'll see you in the morning. Try a stunt like that again and see where it takes you." The bastard walked out of his office and left for the night.

When I turned around, the small gold clock on his desk read 4:28. You've never seen anyone pull on their girdle so fast. I barely made the bus, running and shouting for it to wait. If thoughts could kill, the man would not have made it home in his fancy Lincoln. He would have died of "natural causes" before his wife could serve him his meatloaf.

~*~

Tess grinned, even through her shock. Nana's funny, sassy personality shone through her writing, even if the content was the last thing Tess would ever have expected.

It was definitely a lot to take in. Olivia had been living a secret life for who knew how long?

Though Tess still felt a little guilty over violating her late grandmother's privacy, now that she had started, there was no way she could stop until she'd read every last line. She was glad she'd been the one to discover the journals. Her mom and sister would have been horrified—end of story.

Nana had kept plenty of secrets for Tess. This was the least she could do for her. Nana had never told anyone about the time Tess had shoplifted in fourth grade and gotten caught. She had stared at that Barbie doll for twenty minutes before furtively shoving it down the front of her windbreaker. Terror at what she had done drove her from the store at a run. She couldn't have been more obvious if she'd screamed aloud as she ran, "I stole something. Come get me."

Naturally, the guy behind the counter had run out after her, calling, "Little girl! Little girl!"

She had burst into tears as he caught up with her, and wordlessly held out the stolen Barbie doll. He had taken pity on her, only making her promise not to do that again.

Though she'd gotten off lightly, the guilt at what she'd done had overwhelmed her, as well as a need to confess to someone. Her mother? Even at that young age, Tess sensed that her mother would not have been as forgiving as the man in the store had been. Tess envisioned a spanking at the very least, and quite possibly a huge story blown all out of proportion by the time her father came home, late as usual and smelling of whiskey. Then off would come his belt and little Tess would pay a heavy price for her bad deed.

So she had stayed silent, huddled in her bed in the room she shared with her sister, Stacy. She had confided in no one for three days. But when Saturday finally came and she went to spend the morning with Nana, helping her in her garden and baking cookies, the words had come tumbling out at last, like a wound that had needed lancing to heal.

Tess had known instinctively that Nana wouldn't betray her by telling her parents. Instead, her grandmother had scooped her up in her arms and let her cry out her shame. Stroking her head, she'd asked gently, "And will you do such a silly thing again, Tess sweetheart?"

And as Tess shook her head fervently, Nana kissed her round, wet little cheek and said, "No, I know you won't, and no harm was done, so let's put it behind us, dear. Now, would you like some chocolate chip cookies? I think they're just about done."

Tess sat now, smiling and blinking back tears. How could she reconcile her memories of her dear old Nana with the sexy secretary in the journal, who seemed to be describing the beginnings of a very bizarre love affair?

And Mr. Stevenson. James Stevenson, the man who had called Olivia's home, who was still alive and had maintained contact with his old secretary all these years. Tess toyed with the idea of calling him back. But what would she say?

"I found those diaries and know all about your kinky affair with my grandmother. Explain yourself." What right had she to demand any explanations? Nana had been an adult, making her own decisions decades before Tess was even born.

It was so much to take in.

Maybe Ryan would have some insight.

Should she even tell Ryan?

Tess smiled dreamily. They'd only been seeing each other outside the office for a few weeks now. Ryan Hunter, age twenty-eight, was an attorney just like Tess. They were both known as go-getters at their law firm, though Ryan was further along in his career. Tess had only been with Reilly & Clark for a year, recruited straight out of law school.

Ryan and she had connected while working on a lawsuit together. She'd been instantly attracted to him. He was tall and fit, with arresting green eyes, a straight, elegant nose and a mouth that lifted often into a smile. His light brown hair started out in the mornings slicked back from his forehead, but invariably had flopped forward into his eyes by the end of the long workday.

While he wasn't overtly flirtatious in the office, there had been a definite sexual current humming between them from the minute they'd met. Long days and nights working on the same project had given them time, professionally and otherwise, to check each other out.

When the case was over, Tess was forced to admit she had a full-out crush on the guy. He was good-looking and hard-working, but didn't take himself too seriously, or ever try to put himself above her, either professionally or otherwise. She had managed to suss out that he was single, and while he casually dated, had no steady girlfriend.

She'd been the first one to make the move, inviting him to dinner one Friday, making it seem as if it was a last-minute idea, though she'd been mulling the idea over in her mind for a few days.

That Friday morning she had worn a sexy new thong and matching bra, not that she expected him to see it, but just in case. And, just in case, she made sure the apartment was clean and neat, with fresh sheets on the bed. Not that she expected him to come back to her place, much less get into her bed, but just in case.

When six o'clock rolled around, Ryan was still bent over his work, his sleeves rolled up midway against the sexy muscles of his forearms. His hair had flopped over his forehead as usual, and he had a pen dangling from his mouth. Even in this digital age, his desk was covered in papers.

Unlike Tess, who worked meticulously and neatly on one thing at a time, Ryan liked to spread out over every available surface, balancing twenty things in his head at a time and somehow pulling it all together.

Peeking around his door and trying to tell herself it was cool whichever way it went, Tess had said in a casual tone, "Hey, Ryan. It's Friday. I was thinking of popping over to that new Indian place to check it out. Any chance you'd like to join me?"

She'd held her breath as she waited for his response, telling herself it didn't matter either way, though it did.

To her delight, he replied, "Sure, that's a great idea." He glanced at his watch. "Might as well take a half day—it's Friday, right?" He grinned. "Seriously, though, I'm glad you came to rescue me. I've been staring at the same legal opinion for the past twenty minutes, and my brain is totally fried. Not to mention, I worked through lunch and I'm starving. I could definitely go for some good Indian."

The food was spicy and delicious, and they bantered in an easy, flirtatious way that made Tess's heart skip a beat. When the meal was over, Ryan had turned to Tess and said, "I'd invite you over, but my roommate's girlfriend seems to have kind of moved in lately, and they tend to forget I live there. Last time I came home they both were half-naked and making out on the living room couch. I really need to find a new roommate."

"We could go to my place," Tess ventured, butterflies fluttering in her stomach.

"Sounds like a plan," Ryan agreed with a smile. He followed her in his car to her neighborhood, which was only a few miles from the restaurant.

To her surprise, and perhaps a little to her chagrin, Ryan didn't make any immediate moves on her. Instead, they'd sat together in her living room and just talked. Ryan really seemed to want to know her, which was definitely a refreshing change from most guys she'd dated.

They'd talked for hours, sharing stories about their childhoods, their families, their lives, and Tess felt as if they'd been friends forever. As if by tacit agreement, neither of them talked much about past relationships, which was fine with Tess. When talk had turned to Nana, Ryan had held Tess in his arms, soothing away her tears.

She had expected him to make a move at that point, using the tenderness of the moment to shift the mood, seguing from a chaste, brotherly kiss to a lover's kiss.

When he hadn't, she had been at once impressed and annoyed. She liked that he was a gentleman and hadn't taken advantage of her tears, but weren't they on a date? She'd been too shy to make her own move, however, and the moment had passed.

The conversation slowly eased into lighter things, and they gossiped for a few minutes about the people they worked with. Finally, Ryan said, "I've had a fantastic time, Tess. I can't believe we didn't connect before this. I get so bogged down in my work that sometimes I forget what's really important. I'm so glad we did this. Thank you."

He stood and held out his arms. Tess stood too, stepping into his warm embrace, her heart kicking up a notch in anticipation. He had kissed her then, his lips sweet and warm against hers, but only for a moment or two.

Hungry for more, she had wrapped her arms around him, pulling him against her as she pressed her tongue against his lips until they parted.

To her complete frustration, after another moment or two, he dropped his arms and pulled away from her. Instead of asking where the bedroom was, he said, "Can I call you tomorrow? I was going to go in to the office, but I think I'd much rather spend the day with you, unless, of course, you have plans." He had smiled at her, a wide smile that revealed the dimple in his left cheek.

"Sure, that would be great," Tess had agreed, telling herself sternly that he was behaving sensibly, and she should follow suit. Much better to take their time, rather than tumble into a one-night stand they'd both regret on Monday morning.

They spent a wonderful Saturday, sharing breakfast at an outdoor café, moving on to stroll in the botanical gardens, and then taking in a matinee movie and sharing a late lunch. In the movie theater, Ryan had put his arm loosely around her shoulders, and Tess had leaned into him with a happy sigh.

But after the meal, he'd bailed again, claiming it was his mom's birthday and he couldn't get out of going, as much as he would have liked to. At least the goodbye kiss had been long and lingering, leaving her literally weak in the knees.

That night alone in bed, she had masturbated, imagining Ryan naked and rising over her like a Greek god as she rubbed herself to a marginally satisfying orgasm. It was lonely business, but it did the job, at least enough for her to fall asleep.

They barely saw one another over the next week, each of them piled high with caseloads and paperwork. Tess didn't make it home before ten any night except Friday. They did text and speak on the phone every night, but it wasn't until the following Saturday that they managed to reconnect.

Ryan was going to take her out this time, to his favorite Japanese place. Tess, never having tried sushi, was a little leery, but willing. She wore a sexy, short skirt and a silky blouse she knew complemented her hair and coloring. She couldn't remember being this excited to be with someone since… well, ever!

Leaving their shoes at the door, they had sat side by side on silk cushions set directly on the tatami mat in a private room with rice paper walls and a sliding rice paper door. A brightly colored paper lantern hung from the ceiling, throwing off muted, romantic light.

Their waitress was a tiny Asian woman dressed in a kimono. Tess let Ryan do the ordering. The waitress glided out and returned a moment later with hot tea and sake.

The hot rice wine took a little getting used to, but after the third small cup, Tess was feeling no pain. The waitress returned after a while with a beautiful plate of sushi rolls and sashimi that looked more like art than food. Ryan had smiled at the woman and said something in Japanese. The waitress had smiled broadly, nodding and bowing as she retreated.

"Wow," Tess had said, "do you know Japanese?"

"You just heard the extent of it," Ryan had laughed. "I said thank you, that looks delicious." He picked up a pair of chopsticks. "Let me show you how to eat it. I hope you'll love it as much as I do."

He gestured toward the artfully arranged fish and rice. "You should try the tuna first. It's nice and mild." He picked up a small bowl and lifted a bit of the pale orange vegetable. "You take a little of this, this is pickled ginger"—he placed it on the piece of sushi—"and a little of this green stuff, which is called wasabi. It's a kind of horseradish, and you have to be careful not to use too much or you'll get what I call a wasabi rush."

Tess picked up her chopsticks, hoping she'd somehow manage to pick up a piece without making a complete fool of herself. But, to her relief, Ryan said, "Contrary to some American misperceptions, sushi is considered finger food in Japan." He picked up the sushi in his fingers and held it out to Tess. "Here you go—food for the gods."

He brought his hand closer to her mouth, his green eyes

smoldering as if the two of them were about to have sex instead of food. The room was charged with sudden, electric tension, and Tess's lips parted of their own accord, her eyes locked on Ryan's. His fingers grazed her mouth as he placed the sushi on her tongue.

Tess chewed, trying to ignore the fact she was eating raw fish. To her delighted surprise, an explosion of flavors burst on her tongue—spicy, sweet, salty and delicious, with absolutely nothing fishy about it.

"Wow," she'd enthused. "This is great. I had no idea."

Ryan prepared himself a piece and ate it. Tess started to reach for another piece, but Ryan stopped her with a hand on her bare thigh that sent a rush of heat over her skin. "I'll feed you, Tess. Your only job is to take what I give you."

A strange shudder moved through her at his words, and she had the thrilling feeling he was talking about more than the sushi.

The food was wonderful, and they ordered twice more. Along the way, she lost count of how many small bottles of sake they'd consumed. While Ryan didn't seem in the least tipsy, Tess was definitely feeling its effects by the end of the meal. "That stuff is stronger than you realize," she had remarked. "I don't even know if I can stand up."

Ryan rested his hand lightly on her thigh as he drove her back to her place, and Tess's entire body was thrumming with barely controlled lust. He parked and moved quickly around the car to open the door, which charmed her.

They walked arm in arm to the door of her apartment building. She punched in the code to release the front door and Ryan pulled it open, but made no move to follow her inside. "I had a great time tonight, Tess," he said with a smile.

"Wait, what?" Tess had blurted, alcohol loosening her tongue. "Aren't you coming up? What the hell, Ryan? How long am I supposed to wait for you? What is this, the eighteenth century? Don't you want to fuck me?" As soon as the words had tumbled, uncensored, out of her mouth, she'd blushed to the roots of her hair.

Ryan had just laughed. "Of course I do. Are you kidding me? I've wanted to since I first sat across from you in the conference room when we were working on that case together. Even ignoring the fact we work together and that could get sticky, here's the thing, see..." He'd paused, sobering. "I'll just tell you straight out. I have the bad habit of jumping into bed too soon. It's great for a while, but it usually fizzles out when we figure out all we really have in common is sex."

He had put his hands on her shoulders and stared deep into her eyes. "This feels different, Tess. We've got something, you and me. This time I've sworn to myself not to blow it. I don't want to ruin things by fucking you first and getting to know you later."

Tess had stared back. She was still drunk, but it wasn't the wine that spurred her on. She had to have him, and she was done waiting, end of story. She'd crossed her arms and shaken her head. "Sorry, dude. Not going for it. Feeding me with your fingers like that was definite foreplay, and you don't want to leave a girl frustrated, do you? Either you come upstairs with me this instant and make passionate love to me, or I'm going to have to rape you right here and now."

Ryan had stared at her, his mouth falling open in surprise and, even through the fog of the sake, she suddenly feared she'd gone too far.

But then a slow, sensual smile had lifted his lips. "All right then. We can't have you arrested for sexual assault—you might be disbarred."

Tess didn't remember much after that, at least not the mechanics of going up in the rickety elevator and tumbling into her apartment. What she did remember was the first time he'd entered her—his cock hard and perfect as he lifted his chiseled body over her.

He had made love to her with a kind of wild, exhilarating

desperation that had both thrilled and almost frightened her. Though his kisses had been tender, he'd ravished her in the bed, thrusting inside her as he held her wrists above her head in a strong, dominant grip. She had been completely captive beneath him, at his mercy.

And she'd loved every second of it.

They'd made love all night, and she lost count of her orgasms, which he pulled from her with his cock, his fingers and his mouth, until she was nothing but raw, gasping sensation. He seemed instinctively to know just how far to take her until she was teetering over a sharp, sensual edge. Then he would pull her back, denying her the release she craved.

For Tess, the turn-on was as much what he withheld as what he gave. Ryan played her like an instrument, until she was burning with passion, her entire being focused entirely on him and what he was doing to her.

Finally exhausted, they'd lain together in a tangled tumble of limbs, the scent of sex ripe in the air, too spent to speak or even move. "Tess," Ryan had finally murmured, pulling her into his arms. "I have a confession to make."

Tess had stiffened, suddenly alert. Was this where he admitted he actually had a girlfriend waiting at home, or worse, a wife? Was that why he'd never talked about past relationships?

"Yes?" she managed to murmur back, trying to keep her voice calm.

"I think I'm falling in love with you," he said. Then he laughed, the joy in the sound like sunlight warming Tess from the inside out.

She laughed in response. "That's okay. We're even, because I think I'm falling in love with you, too."

Chapter 4

When Tess woke, Ryan lay sprawled beside her in the bed, his arm flung casually over her midriff, his lips slightly parted, his hair rumpled. She eased carefully from under his arm and slipped out of the bed.

After a quick shower, Tess smiled at her image in the mirror as she toweled herself dry. Ryan was the best thing ever to enter her life. How she wished she could have introduced him to Nana. They would have loved each other instantly, she was sure of it.

When she came out of the bathroom, Ryan hadn't moved. Letting him sleep, she went into the kitchen to make coffee. Pulling some croissants from the freezer, she heated them and prepared a tray with mugs of coffee and the warm croissants.

Ryan opened his eyes as she entered the bedroom. "Hey, sexy," he said, a slow, sleepy smile moving over his face. He hoisted himself into a sitting position against the headboard, his eyes now focused on the tray. "Wow, a beautiful naked woman, incredibly hot sex *and* hot coffee. Have I died and gone to heaven?"

Tess laughed. "If so, I'm right there with you, babe." She set down the tray on the nightstand and as she did so, she noticed the stack of Olivia's journals. Again she wondered—should she share them with Ryan?

She handed him a mug of coffee and a plate with a croissant, and slipped back into bed beside him. She had thought she'd keep Olivia's secrets to herself, but Ryan was fast becoming her significant other.

Based on the intense, sexy, alpha-male way he had made love to her, he would certainly understand and even applaud Olivia's D/s explorations. Tess doubted he would be judgmental or negative, but were the diaries hers to share?

Then again, Tess herself had already violated Olivia's privacy with what she'd read so far. Rather than being horrified by her grandmother's words from so long ago, it was as if Tess had stumbled onto a secret language—one that spoke directly to her heart.

What had Olivia said about Mr. Stevenson?

It's like he was speaking some secret language to me. Some language I didn't know I understood.

And Ryan speaks those same words to me, Tess thought. *He would understand the language, because we all four share it—that unlikely pair from long ago, and Ryan and me today.*

At that moment, she made her decision. She picked up the first journal and said, "I've got something really interesting to show you."

"Oh, yeah? And what is that?"

She told him about her discovery, giving him a thumbnail sketch of the Nana she knew compared to the woman who had written the astonishing account of budding sexual discovery.

Ryan listened, amazement registering on his face as Tess described what she had found. Then he grinned roguishly, his eyes twinkling. Turning toward her, he drew his finger along her cheek, his gaze burning into her. "Just imagine what that must have been like for her. Making dinner and helping the kids with their homework and having boring, duty sex with your husband on the one hand, while at work a secret world of sexual submission and increasingly bizarre demands is opening up for you. Sounds pretty damn hot to me." His expression softened suddenly with concern. "It must be strange for you, though, knowing it was your grandmother who penned those words."

"Especially at first," Tess agreed. "I guess you don't really think of your parents and grandparents as having lives outside what you've always known, which is pretty self-centered. I've come to think of her as Olivia when I read the journals, not as my grandmother. She's more like a friend I would have liked to know."

Ryan had nodded. "That makes sense. Are you going to let me read them?"

"Yes. I've only read part of the first one myself. I've been so busy at work and"—she flashed an impish grin—"other things. I've been kind of parceling it out, savoring each entry. You can read up to where I left off, and then we can read it together. How's that?"

"Sounds great," Ryan agreed.

Tess drank her coffee and ate her croissant as Ryan read. After a while, he looked up. "That Mr. Stevenson is a piece of work, huh?"

"He is," Tess agreed with a laugh. "He's still alive, you know. He called the house."

"No kidding? So they were still going at it hot and heavy in their eighties?"

Tess shrugged. "I don't know about that. He didn't even know she'd died, so I kind of doubt it." She gave Ryan a brief account of the phone call. "I've been wondering if I should call him back. He hung up before I could tell him much." She paused, adding, "He did seem strongly affected by her death though. He sounded pretty broken up."

"His wife may still be alive," Ryan replied. "We don't know anything about his circumstances now."

Tess thought about it, nodding slowly. "Yeah. I'd love to talk to the guy sometime, if I could get up the nerve. I jotted down the number from her landline caller ID, just in case."

"Good thinking, counselor. Keep the evidence for future discovery by the court. Can we read another entry? How about you read it out loud for me?"

~*~

October 30, 1961

Well, he waited a whole week, but Mr. Stevenson finally asked to see the beautiful undergarments he'd bought me. To be fair, the man was out of town on a business trip Thursday and Friday, and I only worked half days a result. I still wore the sexy panties and garter belt every day. It made me feel closer to him.

I have to admit, there's something very sexy about sliding those stockings slowly up my legs in the bathroom at work. Plus, there's the ritual aspect of it. Mr. Stevenson says rituals are important, and will become more a part of my training as time goes on. My training! Can you imagine? Like I'm some kind of prize show horse.

But no. Let's be honest, Livvie. It's not like that. It's something very different. Something dark and dangerous and exciting that I still don't really understand, but that I am somehow compelled to obey.

This morning as I was getting ready in the bathroom at work, I had a brief fantasy that he opened the door while I was putting the stockings on and just stood there, watching. I imagined the two of us in some kind of sultry film noir, my leg raised provocatively as I eased the soft silk up a firm calf, and he watched, mesmerized.

Well, that didn't happen, of course. But about a half hour after he arrived this morning, he called me in, his quiet but commanding tone sending a shiver over my skin.

"Olivia."

He was seated at his desk when I entered the office, and I stood in front of him, trying to appear calm. I had missed our daily interactions more than I would care to admit.

"Take off your skirt and slip."

Just like that. No building up to it. Just take your skirt right off in front of your boss.

"Excuse me?" I said, to buy time.

"Do I need to repeat myself? Am I unclear?"

"Well, um, it's just you haven't asked that before, I mean, not since that punishment, and I don't think I've incurred any infractions—"

"You have now. Don't question me. Do as you're told."

Well, I did, all the time thinking, *be careful what you wish for*. You wanted him to look at your garters, and now he's doing it, so what's your problem? Yes, I did want it—I'll admit that straight out. I think I hesitated because it was sudden, so unexpected, and I felt rather shy. No man but Frank has ever seen me like that.

But he sat there, a calm look on his handsome face, as if what he were asking was nothing out of the ordinary.

This is it, I thought. No turning back now. The side zipper stuck a little and my fingers were trembling as I fumbled with the little tag. I pushed the skirt down my legs, hoping against hope I wouldn't trip in my heels and make a fool of myself. I lay my skirt and slip over the back of a chair and then stood there in my garters and stockings, and of course my underpants, bra and blouse, nervous as a colt as I fidgeted from foot to foot.

Instead of looking pleased, or at least lecherous, the man looked horrified. I blushed from the tip of my ears down to my toes. How dare he look at me that way? I mean, I may be no spring chicken, but I'm not *that* hard on the eyes.

But apparently *I* wasn't the problem.

"What is that ridiculous underwear?" he demanded.

Can you imagine? They're just nice practical cotton underpants. Does he think I have drawers full of skimpy satin panties like those young models are wearing? I'm a grown woman. I've had three children. I retorted something along those lines.

He smiled slightly, but his tone remained stern. "Olivia, I don't want you to wear that white cotton underwear at the office ever again, do you understand? It goes the way of the girdle. I will have another package prepared for you at Slone's tomorrow."

Beyond the humiliation and irritation at his insulting my perfectly fine underpants, I was miffed—I'll admit it. He hadn't said a word about my legs, which I know are still nice, or the garters, or the fact that I had obeyed him without protest and taken off the skirt.

I tell you, the man is driving me to distraction.

Later: Just time to write a few words here. Mr. Stevenson called me in again and gave me detailed instructions about Slone's. I'm to go over as soon as they open in the morning. I'm to ask for Miss Wilson and tell her I'm there for a fitting. He says she will tell me exactly what to do and I must obey her to the letter, no matter what she instructs me to do.

My initial reaction was to demand just what he meant by obeying this woman to the letter. What "orders" could a saleslady possibly have for me? Aren't I the customer? I very nearly asked, too, but a look from Mr. Stevenson kept me from forming the words.

He went on to say he will receive a full report from her about my actions and behavior, and he's confident I will do just exactly as I am told. I don't mind saying—I'm nervous as a cat now. Just what am I letting myself in for?

I could just refuse.

But I know I won't.

~*~

Ryan gave a low whistle. "Man, this stuff is incredible, Tess. I feel like I'm getting to know Olivia, and she's definitely someone I would have loved to meet."

"I never met this particular Olivia," Tess replied. "I would have liked to meet her, too."

Ryan nodded. "Her writing style is really engaging. It's so hot but so funny, all at the same time." He shook his head. "Imagine if that dude tried something like that today at the office."

"Hashtag Me Too, right?" Tess agreed with a laugh. "Though clearly whatever was going on between them was consensual. Olivia was definitely into it."

"Sure, why wouldn't she be? Imagine how it must have been for her, Tess." Ryan's voice deepened, and the room was suddenly charged with sexual tension. "It's hot to be dommed by a man who understands your intrinsic need to submit." He brought his arm around Tess's shoulders and pulled her close to him. He cupped her breast, his fingers closing around her nipple. He squeezed it, lightly at first, then harder.

Intrinsic need to submit.

The words bypassed her brain, sending a sudden, hot jolt directly to her pussy. His grip was tight on her nipple, the sensation a confusion of pain and pleasure. Startled at her own powerful reaction, she focused instead on the obvious as she blurted, "That hurts, Ryan."

"But it's a good pain, isn't it, Tess?"

Tess swallowed hard, unable to respond, a flush of heat moving over her skin.

Ryan released her nipple and pulled his arm from around her shoulders. Taking the journal from her hands, he set it on the nightstand. Turning to face her, he lifted her chin as he lowered his mouth to hers.

The kiss was both tender and commanding, and Tess melted against the pillow as their tongues entwined, her body yielding and ready for him.

But when he finally pulled away, instead of making love to her, he picked up the journal again and said, "Lie back and close your eyes. I'm going to read the next entry to you."

~*~

October 31, 1961

This may have been the strangest day so far. I left at 9:45 in the morning, right in the middle of our workday, as Mr. Stevenson had instructed. The shop is only two blocks over and the morning was pleasant, but I barely noticed, intent on my mission. They buzzed me in, and I went right over to the counter and asked for Miss Wilson.

A plump, pleasant-looking young woman came out from the back and held out her hand to me. "You must be Olivia. It's a pleasure to meet you. Please come back to our private fitting area. I'm all ready for you."

As we were walking through the boutique, I was struck by the woman's usage of my first name, but maybe that's all Mr. Stevenson had told her. She unlocked a door that was covered in brocaded pink satin, very posh, and gestured for me to go into what turned out to be a rather large fitting room with floor-to-ceiling mirrors hung on all the walls. A number of satin undergarments had been set out on a low counter.

Miss Wilson took a seat on the only chair in the room and looked up at me. "I've brought a few things in for you to try. Mr. Stevenson did give me some direction, but he trusts my discretion." She regarded me with a tilted head for a moment, cupping her chin and tapping her mouth while I stood there, as self-conscious as a schoolgirl.

"Now that I see you"—she rose from the chair and walked over to the counter— "I think we should try this one, and this, and this." She picked up a pair of the underwear and handed them to me.

I stared at her. Was she suggesting I try on the panties with her just standing there watching me? I didn't want to be rude and order her to get out, so I said instead, "I'm sorry. I don't understand."

"My apologies," she said smoothly, smiling in a rather superior but still kindly way. "Mr. Stevenson instructed me to treat you as usual."

"As usual?" I replied, thoroughly confused. "Usual what?"

She colored very slightly. "He, uh, didn't tell you what to do?"

Now I was the one to blush. "He said to, um, to obey whatever you told me to do." I looked down, my cheeks on fire. What in God's name was I doing there? I very nearly turned on my heel and walked out the pink satin door, Mr. Stevenson's directions be damned.

Miss Wilson touched my arm. "Please, Olivia," she said gently. "There's nothing to be frightened of. I can see this is new for you, and you aren't sure what to expect." She bit her lip and then seemed to come to some kind of decision. "If you'll excuse me a moment, I need to make a quick phone call. Please wait just a moment. I'll be right back." She slipped out of the room, closing the door with a soft click behind her.

Again I thought about just walking out, but I had to admit, the gorgeous lingerie had got my attention. I had never seen anything quite so lovely in my life, and I walked over to the counter to examine it more closely.

The panties were made with heavy satin and edged with exquisite lace, beautifully sewn in creamy beige, black and crimson. I touched the fabric to my cheek, enjoying the smooth, soft slide of it on my skin. I was sure they must cost more than I made in a month. But hey, it was Mr. Stevenson's dime.

She came back, slightly out of breath. "I've talked to Mr. Stevenson, and he explained the uh, newness, of your situation. I understand things better now. Mr. Stevenson says we are to take our time, so don't worry about hurrying back to the office."

Sitting down again, she said, "I'd like you to try on a pair of the underwear so I can assess if the fit and style is right for you." She made no move to get up and leave.

I glanced around, as if a privacy screen had materialized in a corner of the room while I wasn't looking. "Um, right in front of you?"

"Oh," she waved her hand airily, like this was an everyday thing, which perhaps for her, it was. "Don't be shy. This is my profession. I see women in a state of undress all the time. Mr. Stevenson would like you to remove your clothing so I can properly assess the full effect. You can leave on the garter belt, stockings and brassiere, but please do remove everything else."

Talk about baptism by fire!

What the heck was I doing there? Was I really going to strip in front of a stranger and try on sexy panties that I was to wear only at work? Were things moving to a new level between Mr. Stevenson and me? If I obeyed, did that mean I was tacitly agreeing to become Mr. Stevenson' paramour?

We've never even shared a kiss. I call him Mr. Stevenson, for heaven's sake. Yet, there I was, trying on that gorgeous lingerie in front of a stranger, because Mr. Stevenson had commanded it.

My hands are shaking as I write this. God help me, I did it. I took off my things, keeping my burning face averted as I tried on the panties, which included a paper insert to keep them fresh.

She was extremely complimentary, and after a while, I did relax some, though my heart never stopped pounding. I had to admit, I did look pretty darn good in all those mirrors. What in the world would Frank think if he saw me in one of those getups? Maybe I should get something like this for home—might spice up our sex life.

Frank aside, the experience was both strange and thrilling in the extreme. I can hardly wait until Mr. Stevenson calls me in to show him what he paid for. Maybe we're not lovers, but something is definitely going on between us. And I won't lie—it's the most exciting thing that's ever happened to me in my life.

~*~

Tess had kept her eyes closed as Ryan had read aloud to her, but she was clearly listening. Her lovely nipples were round and hard, her hands clenching as the words came to life on the page. A flush had risen on her chest, spreading up over her cheeks, and her lips were softly parted, as if waiting for his kiss.

Ryan had been amused at first at the prospect of reading Tess's grandmother's diary, prepared to dismiss it as casual kink. He hadn't been prepared for the power of that young woman's words reaching out to him from across the decades. While his own sexual fantasies regarding BDSM took a much darker twist, it was clear Olivia "got it"— she understood the potential of dominance and submission on a gut level, even if she lacked experience and knowledge about the lifestyle.

Ryan had had a few serious relationships over the years, but they had fizzled out over time. The girls were perfectly nice—*he'd* been the problem. It wasn't that he wasn't willing, even eager, to find true intimacy with a woman, but with each girl, from the beginning, if he were totally honest, he'd already visualized the ending, aware at least on some level that the essential spark between them was missing.

With Tess, however, it was more than a spark. A flame had ignited between them. He was excited by Tess's powerful reaction not only to Olivia's depictions, but to his subtle dominance over her during sex. It was clear that she, like Olivia, was treading in uncharted territory, but was eager to continue the exploration.

Ryan set the journal down and reached for Tess, taking her in his arms.

She wrapped herself around him, pressing her warm body against his. Her soft breasts were crushed against his chest as he held her close. They kissed for several minutes until Ryan pulled away long enough to murmur, "It's about control, Tess."

"What?" Tess said breathlessly, her lips still parted and shiny with his kisses. Her hair was wild around her face, her pupils dilated. Ryan put his hand lightly on her chest. Her heart was pounding, her breathing ragged and shallow.

"Allowing another person to take erotic control. That's what excited Olivia, and you, too, are feeling its power." He reached for her again, this time pressing her down against the bed as he lifted her arms above her head. Holding both her wrists with one hand, he slipped his other hand between her legs.

Her cunt was wet, her little clit hard as a pea. "Fuck me," she said throatily.

"No."

Tess's eyes flew open. "What?"

It was very probably the first time in her life she'd ever been refused by a man.

"You heard me," Ryan replied with an amused smile, power coursing through his veins like a drug.

Her face twisted into an adorable pout. "Huh? Why not?"

"Because you haven't earned it, Tess."

She frowned and squirmed beneath him. "What are you talking about?"

He held her wrists fast. "I know you want it, but you need to be controlled, don't you, little girl? You're longing to surrender to the right man. To the right Master."

Color rose on Tess's cheeks, her eyes fever bright. "Ryan, I…I don't know what…" Abruptly she turned her head away.

Letting go of one wrist, he reached for her face, gently forcing her to look at him. "You do know," he said with conviction. "We both know. You have permission now, Tess. Permission to accept your true nature. You've been waiting all your life for this." He stared into her eyes, speaking from his heart. "As have I."

Her expression softened. "Yes," she whispered, her body relaxing beneath his. "Yes."

Ryan positioned his rock-hard cock between her thighs. "I'm going to claim you, Tess. I'm going to make you mine in every sense of the word."

She moaned as he nudged the head of his cock into her wet, tight heat. He entered her with a groan. When he sensed she was close, her body trembling, her breathy cries rising with passion, he let go of her wrists and slid his arms beneath her. "Come for me, Tess," he commanded. "Give me everything you've got."

With a sharp cry, she jerked hard beneath him, her cunt spasming as she climaxed, dragging him over the edge along with her.

As their hearts slowed their pounding rhythms, Ryan rolled to his side, pulling her along with him so they were facing one another, his cock still inside her. "I'm going to take control, Tess," he said, looking deep into her eyes. "I'm going to teach you what it is to submit. Do you understand?"

Wordlessly, her eyes wide, she nodded.

Chapter 5

November 7, 1961

It was just a matter of time. I can't fool myself anymore about what is or isn't happening between us. And if this was just a game before, albeit a bizarre one, it has gone beyond that now.

And here's the weird thing. I'm not sorry. I don't feel guilty. I mean, maybe I do a little, or I wouldn't be writing this, I guess. But Frank would never understand the feelings Mr. Stevenson has somehow awakened in me, or planted in me, or whatever he has done. What about Mrs. Stevenson? It's hard to imagine her as a flesh-and-blood person. She's more like a shadowy figure in the background. Perhaps she is his Madonna and I am his whore. Maybe between us, we give him what he needs.

Each day for the past week, I've worn the lovely lingerie he bought for me, and each day, though he has found a reason to use his ruler, it has always been over the skirt. I admit I was both frustrated and relieved by this. Did I expect him to ask me to model it as Miss Wilson had?

Yes, to be honest, I guess I did. You don't buy a woman sexy lingerie and then not want to see it, do you? If you're a normal man, that is. I guess that's my mistake. While I find Mr. Stevenson exciting and even dangerous in a sexy kind of way, I certainly wouldn't describe him as normal.

But I'm digressing.

Here's what happened.

Mr. Stevenson called me in after lunch today. He wasn't behind his desk, but was sitting in a relaxed pose in one of his wing-backed chairs. Without preamble, he said, "I presume you're wearing the lingerie I purchased for you?"

"Yes, Sir," I said, suddenly finding the air in the room to be short of oxygen.

"Show me."

At first, I misunderstood, thinking he meant for me to go get the satin lingerie I keep in a hatbox under the sink in the office bathroom. I almost turned to go and get it when he clarified, "Take off your dress, please." When I didn't react, he added sternly, "Olivia. Do as you're told. Now."

My blood went both hot and cold at once, my heart instantly skittering into a rapid beat. It was the moment I'd been waiting for, but now that it had arrived, did I have the nerve?

I reached back to unzip my dress with trembling fingers. Carefully, I laid it over a chair, keenly aware of Mr. Stevenson's intent gaze.

I stood there in bra, panties, stockings and heels, fidgeting like a schoolgirl in the principal's office, not sure what to do with my arms.

Cool as a cucumber, Mr. Stevenson looked me up and down like he owned me, his eyes raking my body as heat washed over my face and chest. "Very nice," he finally pronounced. "You are beautiful, Olivia."

I'll admit it here. Though I'm sure I was red as a beet, I was ridiculously pleased with his compliment.

He got to his feet and approached me. I could smell his cologne—

something spicy but subtle—and the faint scent of starch on his fine, white shirt. I forgot to breathe as he dipped his head toward me. Very lightly, almost tentatively, he touched his lips to mine.

I stood very still, not quite sure even as it was happening that he was kissing me. But that's what it was. He gave me a kiss. A chaste, closed-mouth kiss, but a kiss nonetheless. Then he brought his arms around me and let his hands rest on my bottom! He stroked the fine satin panties he'd paid for.

A shudder moved through me and my nipples hardened. I longed to put my arms around him, too, but something held me back. I just stood there, frozen in place, a statue for him to fondle.

His hands moved over my body, his fingers warm against my bare back. He took a step back and placed his hand between my legs, cupping my sex over the satin panties.

I thought I was going to faint.

Something odd was going on inside my body—as if some kind of dark, liquid fire had replaced my blood. I was literally burning with desire. My heart was rattling around in my rib cage as we locked eyes. His fingers moved down between my legs, though still over the panties.

A part of me couldn't believe this was happening, but at the same time, what had I expected? Maybe the question wasn't, "How could this be happening?" but rather, "Why has it taken so long?"

Instead of throwing me to the ground in a fit of passion, however, Mr. Stevenson calmly took his seat again, fully in control. Looking up at me, he said in a voice that brooked no argument, "Take off your panties, Olivia."

I was surprised, not so much that he wanted me naked, but that he'd asked me to take off my panties first. I was still wearing my shoes, for heaven's sake. And I would have thought he'd want to see my breasts first.

While I stood there blushing like a fool, he lifted an eyebrow. "Olivia? Did you hear me?"

"I-I-I," I stammered like Norton when Ralph used to yell at him on the *Honeymooners* (Frank's favorite show in the fifties. Heaven help me, what would Frank think of what I'm doing? I must be out of my mind.)

A half smile lifted Mr. Stevenson's lips. "Your modesty is charming, but I have given you a specific task, and I expect you to execute it—that is, if you are still my submissive, obedient secretary."

I didn't move. It wasn't that I didn't want to, I simply couldn't find the will to make my hands obey.

"Of course the choice is ultimately yours," he said after a beat. "You will choose either to obey or refuse." He exhaled the hint of a sigh. "I've enjoyed our developing relationship and had believed you were ready for the next phase, but you're under no compulsion to continue. You've done an admirable job as my secretary, and if that's all you wish to remain, I'll be happy to provide two weeks salary and whatever references you need to procure a similar post." He paused meaningfully before adding, "Do I make myself clear?"

He did. Crystal clear.

Strip or you're fired.

That was the bottom line, wasn't it? And yet, why should I take offense? I'd gone along with each bizarre, thrilling, strange request to this point. I'd fantasized endlessly about a torrid love affair, even as I'd been terrified by the thought. And now, here we were.

I knew one thing for sure—I didn't want to quit my job. I didn't want to be fired. I didn't want two weeks of pay and a reference letter, and it wasn't about the money. I wanted the thrill of whatever had been going on between us to continue.

I wanted him.

And I believed his threat. I didn't doubt for a moment that he'd let me go, just like that. The thought of never seeing my dark, dangerous, peculiar boss again left me bereft. Yes—that's the word. My life would be bleaker without him in it. The thrill, the verve, the excitement, would be gone.

But it was even more than that. Standing there practically naked in front of a man who was not my husband was thrilling. I was excited—sexually aroused (let's call a spade a spade, shall we?)—in a way I've never been in my life. And not only that, I didn't want to let Mr. Stevenson down. I wanted to please him.

And so, I did it. My eyes on his, I pushed my panties down my legs and kicked them aside, my heart beating so hard I could hear it. But I stood my ground, lifting my chin with determination, refusing to cover myself or run away.

He rose from his chair, his eyes hooded in a way that sent a pleasant, thrilling shiver down my spine. He really is quite a good-looking man. He approached me again, and this time, when his lips touched mine, his tongue slipped into my mouth.

His arms went around me, and he unclasped my bra with sure fingers. I kept on kissing him, a part of me thinking if I didn't acknowledge what was happening, it wouldn't count. He let the bra fall between us as I pushed close against him, shy about his seeing my breasts.

Reaching down, he cupped my now bare sex. My impulse was both to push him away and pull him closer. I was terrified but also more excited than I've ever been in my life.

He stroked me, pressing a finger inside me, moving over me in a way I've never been touched. I don't even have words for it. It was like this warm, dark, buttery feeling spreading from his fingertips through my body, leaving me weak in the knees. His touch was at once as soft as butterfly wings, yet at the same time firm and insistent, as if he had every right to do what he was doing.

Until that moment, I'd never really understood what all the hoopla was about. Let's face it, sex with Frank has always been about Frank. I mean, I know that's normal and all, as men have a higher sex drive and what have you, but my husband has never touched me the way Mr. Stevenson did.

A part of me whispered that what he was doing was dirty. But you know what? I don't really believe that. What's wrong with giving and experiencing such pleasure?

Dropping his hand, he led me to the couch and pressed me gently down. He knelt between my legs and placed his hands on my thighs. There I was, decked out in garters, stockings, heels and nothing else, while this fully clothed man who was not my husband stared down at my privates.

I could have died.

Then he placed his hand again on my aching sex, and God help me, I moaned like an animal in heat. He began to move his fingers again in that magic, astonishing way and I knew I was heading toward something powerful. Right or wrong be damned, I didn't want him to stop. Ever.

I began to pant, unable to control myself, my whole body on fire with pure, unadulterated lust.

"Yes," he said softly. "That's it, Olivia. Give yourself to me in this way. I demand it."

Something clenched inside me, hard and tight as a ticking time bomb. Then, all at once—wham! I exploded into a powerful climax that lifted me right out of myself.

I have wondered from time to time if I'd had an orgasm with Frank, but I understand now I'd had no idea—simply no idea.

I lay back sprawled against his sofa, any trace of modesty vanquished by the raw pleasure coursing through me. He just watched me with those blue, impenetrable eyes of his, like I was some kind of specimen or experiment. It was disconcerting, but also, in a strange way, deeply exciting.

After a while, without a word exchanged between us about what had just happened, Mr. Stevenson got to his feet. Holding out his hand, he hoisted me upright. "You may dress and return to your desk, Olivia."

Just like that, I was dismissed.

And here's the thing—I didn't protest. I didn't ask him if we were now officially having an affair. I didn't wonder that he'd remained dressed during the whole bizarre, astonishing event. I was still reeling from the orgasm, the first real orgasm of my life.

Truth be told, I wanted another one, right then and there.

Am I turning into some kind of crazed nymphomaniac? I wish I could talk to someone about this. Another woman. A friend. Can you imagine Betty's face if I tried to tell her any of this? She'd think I needed to be committed to a psychiatric facility. Electro-shock therapy would definitely be called for.

It's not just that I'm having an affair with my boss. Because I can no longer pretend that's not what's happening here. But it's so much more. This burning intensity I feel inside, this heightened feeling, this passion—it's beyond words. Mr. Stevenson has awoken something in me. Something I didn't know I possessed, didn't know I needed.

That's it.

I *need* what he offers, even if I don't entirely understand it.

~*~

"Hey there. You have a second?" Ryan stood in the doorway of Tess's office.

Just the sound of his voice quickened her heart. She looked up and smiled at her new lover. "Sure, what's up?"

He looked crisp and fresh in his suit and tie, his hair slicked back, his strong jaw smooth. You'd never know by looking at him that they'd spent half the night making wild, passionate love, stopping only when exhaustion claimed them. She had awoken in his arms, her cheek resting on his chest, happiness blooming inside her before she was even fully conscious.

They'd stayed up late, taking turns reading Olivia's increasingly astonishing journal to one another between bouts of lovemaking. Tess no longer thought of the woman who had penned those words so long ago as her Nana. She was instead becoming a friend, someone Tess would have loved to know, not as her grandmother, but as a person.

Though her situation with Ryan was quite different, without all the restrictions and taboos that pair had been facing, it was fascinating how Olivia and she were embarking on parallel paths in terms of the exploration of their inner submissive sexual desires.

Ryan stepped into the office and handed Tess a small, thin book bound in leather. Their fingers touched as she took the gift, an electric spark passing between them.

"What's this?" she asked, looking down at the clearly much-read book, its cover worn soft, the pages inside yellowed with age. She read the title—*Charlotte's Awakening*—which was stamped onto the leather in gold lettering, some of the letters partially flaked away.

"It's something I've had for a long time. I probably read it a dozen times over the years. I found it in a used bookstore when I was a freshman in college. Though it's not exactly a love story, the message in it is very powerful, and it resonated with me. I've never shared it with anyone else, but I want you to have it."

"Wow," Tess said, touched he was giving her something clearly important to him. "What's it about?"

His smile was enigmatic. "Read it and see." He glanced at his watch. "I have court in a hour. I have to get going. I'll see you later tonight, okay?"

"Sure, yes. That would be great."

He bent down and gave her a quick kiss, and then he was gone.

Tess stroked the book's soft cover and opened it, her curiosity piqued. She hadn't intended to read it until she got home, but the first sentence grabbed her attention, and she tumbled headlong into the story.

"The first time I saw him, the word Sir rose like an offering to my lips, and the knees of my heart dropped into a kneeling pose before him…"

Three hours later, Tess closed the book with a sigh. She had done more than enough billable hours that week, but even if she'd been in the middle of an emergency case, she doubted she would have been able to put the book down.

Copyrighted in 1960, around the same time as Olivia's real life adventures were beginning, *Charlotte's Awakening* was an erotic, sexually explicit story, written in sparse but powerful language that spoke directly to Tess's darkest desires. Charlotte, a young woman in England at the end of the nineteenth century, takes a lover who exerts his dominant will on her, teaching her to submit in every aspect of her life. While not romantic, the book was deeply erotic.

The male protagonist, Sir Jonathan, was strangely cold and

forbidding, but Charlotte's immersion into complete submission and subjugation at the hands of her lover, and at the hands of the men he chose to share her with, made Tess's face burn and her pussy throb.

Though Tess disapproved intellectually of Charlotte permitting herself to be treated as a sex object, used and debased as it pleased her "Master," Tess's heart, body and soul responded to the story on a visceral, intense level that left her breathless. As Tess read the stark descriptions of forced sex, intense bondage and erotic torture, she became dizzy with barely controlled lust, her nipples aching, her panties soaked. Unable to help herself, she slipped her hand into her panties, rubbing herself to several quick orgasms as she lost herself in the story.

Finally closing the book, she sat back, wrung out from the experience as if she, not Charlotte, had experienced the dark, erotic adventure. The ending was upsetting, with Charlotte's lover ultimately abandoning her when he was "done with her." The final scene, with Charlotte bent over her needlework by an insufficient coal fire in the tiny room to which she had been relegated, was heartbreaking. Even with the unsatisfactory ending, however, the tale had lodged itself deep in Tess's psyche.

As she gathered her things to leave the office, she thought about a younger Ryan reading these words, and about his statement that he'd read it a dozen times over the years. Clearly, he had been as affected as she was by the novel, but what was his take on it? He was no Sir Jonathan, thank goodness. Where that man was cold and forbidding, Ryan was warm, loving and even playful. But the two men shared an underlying dominance, a basic need to control and command, which spoke directly to the submissive Tess was finally beginning to embrace inside herself.

Just as she was heading out of her office, her cell phone dinged. Pulling it from her purse, she saw it was from Ryan.

Out of court. You home yet or still at work?

Just leaving now.

Great. I'm heading over to Nemo's. Meet me there for a drink and a bite to eat?

Sure. See you in fifteen.

Nemo's was a popular restaurant favored by young professionals and office workers. It was within walking distance from the office, and Tess decided she could use the fresh air. Leaving her car in the building's garage, she stepped out into the cool evening, her sensible heels clicking on the concrete, her briefcase banging at her side.

She made her way through the usual throng to the bar where Ryan sat, jacket off, tie loosened, hair in his eyes. Miraculously, he'd managed to save her a seat on the barstool next to his. He stood as she approached and gave her a quick hug. Once they were seated and her drink order placed, he swiveled toward her. "You read the book?"

"Yes," Tess admitted, a flush moving over her skin. "It was…powerful."

He placed his hand on her thigh, his touch instantly electrifying her senses. The noise and chaos of the crowd around them was like a privacy screen in a way—no one paid them the slightest attention. "I want to take you there, Tess," he murmured softly in his deep, sexy voice. "I want to teach you to submit—not like Sir Jonathan and Charlotte, but in our own way, the way we determine together." He caught her in his gaze, his green eyes like crystal-cut emerald and black onyx. "Do you want that, Tess?"

"Yes," she whispered, her breath caught in her throat, her nipples painfully erect. "Yes, please."

He nodded slowly. "Good. I want you to go to the restroom and remove your panties. Then come back to me."

His words penetrated the sensual web he had woven around her with his sexy words. "Wait. What?"

"You didn't hear me?"

"I heard you but—"

"No buts, Tess. You say you want what I'm offering. Prove it. Do as you're told." He reached for a tendril of her hair that had fallen into her face and tucked it behind her ear as he said, more gently this time, "Trust me, darling. I know you want this as much as I do."

"Yes," she admitted, only able to speak in a whisper. "Yes, okay."

In something of a daze, she slid off the stool and made her way to the restrooms at the back of the restaurant, taking her purse with her. She had to wait a moment for an open stall, and while she waited, she looked at herself in the mirror, wondering if her thrilled confusion and excitement showed in her face. But other than her heightened color, which could have been from drink or heat as much as anything, she looked like her normal old self.

She slipped into a vacant stall and pulled down her panties, still damp from her reading, and shoved them into her purse. She returned to the bar, where her drink was waiting. Just as she was about to sit down, Ryan placed his hand lightly on her arm. "Lift your skirt and sit directly on the leather. I cleaned it with the disinfectant spray I keep in my briefcase for my jail visits, so you don't need to worry in that regard."

"You're kidding, right?"

He frowned. "Do I look like I'm kidding?"

Slowly, she shook her head. She could have easily refused. She could have tossed her head with a laugh and told him she wasn't interested in playing these silly games. But, the truth was, they didn't feel silly. She was deeply excited, her heart hammering in her chest, her entire body on fire with lust.

"No, Sir," she whispered, consciously echoing Charlotte's first words to her Master.

With a glance around her, she lifted her skirt and settled herself carefully against the cool leather stool.

Ryan was watching her with hooded eyes. He leaned over and kissed her lightly on the lips. "You please me," he murmured, and his words sent a warm jolt of pleasure through her. "Your bare ass on the seat is a symbol of your willingness to submit to me."

Again, Tess's intellect tried to intervene, ordering her to reply with indignant flippancy to his words, but her heart, body and soul ignored the protests. This was what she had been born for—what she'd longed for without knowing the words or understanding the vocabulary.

When their name was called, the hostess led them to a small booth toward the back of the room. After she'd gone, Ryan pulled a small spray bottle from his jacket and sprayed the leather bench, using one of the cloth napkins to wipe it clean.

"You enter first," he said, taking a step back so Tess could move past him. "Bare ass on the leather. I'll sit beside you."

Tess slid into the booth and scooted along the bench. Once Ryan was seated beside her, she lifted herself and hiked her skirt so her bare bottom made contact with the bench, glad for the shield of Ryan's body.

She felt at once vulnerable and empowered, and thrilled deep in her bones at Ryan's taking such charge of her. She glanced shyly at him, but he wasn't looking at her. He was busy perusing the menu, and she picked hers up as well, though she had a hard time focusing on the options.

"Want to share a pizza?" Ryan asked as if there was nothing unusual about what was going on.

Nemo's was famous for their huge wood-burning oven and the

fabulous pizzas they produced. "Sure," Tess agreed, suddenly aware she was starving. "How about a pepperoni, sausage, mushroom and onion with extra cheese?"

"Sounds perfect to me," he agreed with a grin.

After a waiter came to refresh their drinks and take their order, Ryan said quietly, "Are you wet, Tess?"

"Um," she hedged, embarrassed to admit the truth.

He fixed her with his intense gaze. "Touch yourself and tell me."

Her heart skipping several beats, Tess let her thighs part. She reached beneath the table and under her skirt. As she stroked herself lightly, an electric jolt of pleasure hurtled through her body.

"Tell me," he urged.

"Yes," she whispered.

"Yes, what?"

"Yes, I'm wet...Sir."

Sir. Just as for Olivia, and just as for Charlotte, it felt...right.

"I want you to masturbate, Tess. Right here. Right now. Do it for me."

Forget grey. She was certain her face was fifty shades of red. At the same time, she was wildly aroused. Charlotte's dark story still lingered in her mind, and Ryan's powerful, sexy domination was an irresistible aphrodisiac.

Giving herself over to her need, Tess rubbed herself, her natural juices more than enough lubrication. With Ryan right beside her, his strong thigh touching hers, it wasn't long before a climax began to build inside. She began to pant, trying to stay as quiet and unobtrusive as she could as her fingers flew over her sex. Closing her eyes, she focused on her task, desperate to finish before the waiter's return.

"Tess, stop."

She was vaguely aware of Ryan's command, but too far-gone to obey. Just a few more strokes. She needed it. She had to have it.

"Tess, you need to stop." His voice was more urgent, but at that moment, she couldn't have stopped if she'd wanted to. The orgasm caught her by the throat and slammed her to the ground as she rocked in the booth, unable to stifle her low, husky moan.

When she opened her eyes, Ryan was looking at her with an amused smile. The waiter, tray in hand, was gaping at her open-mouthed, frozen with shocked surprise.

"Oh my god," Tess gasped, slamming her legs together. *Why didn't you tell me he was there!* she wanted to demand, but then, he had tried, hadn't he? She'd ignored him, too intent on taking her pleasure.

Ryan turned to the waiter and said smoothly, "You can just leave the drinks, thanks. We're good."

"Oh. Yeah. Uh, right," the young man said, a grin suddenly moving over his face that made Tess blush again. "Your pizza should be right up."

Ryan lifted his eyebrows after the guy had gone. "See what happens when you don't obey my command?" he teased with a laugh. "Though, I have to say, you probably made that dude's day. Shit, his whole week."

In spite of her chagrin, Tess laughed too.

Ryan put his arm around her, leaning close. "You're so fucking hot, Tess. I can't wait to get you home."

Chapter 6

November 13, 1961

Mr. Stevenson is the second man I've ever been intimate with.

Listen to me with my euphemisms, even here in my private diary.

Speak plainly, Livvie. Say what you mean.

Okay.

He's the second man I've had sex with.

Yes. It's true. I made love with a man who is not my husband.

Was it making love? Is that what you'd call it? I have no earthly idea.

My head is in a muddle. Maybe if I write this all down, it will become clearer as I go.

When Mr. Stevenson suggested I accompany him on his business trip, I honestly didn't think Frank would go for it, even though Betty promised to get the kids after school and make sure they were up and ready for the bus in the morning. I wasn't even sure myself how I felt about it. I've never been away from them overnight, except when they go to summer camp.

Though it was only for one night, I warned Mr. Stevenson it was unlikely, and he nodded his understanding. Though he did add that I would be amply compensated, given the inconvenience. I think that's what motivated Frank, to be brutally honest. I'll admit here, I know how to play Frank, and by acting very low-key and hesitant—I wasn't sure it was a good idea, what about the children—I manipulated him into feeling he was the one advocating for the trip and I was the reluctant one.

"We'll be fine," he'd assured me. "We can make it on our own for one night without Mom, can't we, kids?"

"Will you bring us a toy?" Frank Jr. had piped up. My assurances that I would clinched the deal. Toys for all, and a nice bonus check to boot.

I seem to be avoiding the task at hand, which is to put down what happened. What "transpired," as Mr. Stevenson is fond of saying.

It's funny how I always think of him as Mr. Stevenson. Does his wife call him James, or something more endearing, like Jim or Jimmy? I can't see him as a Jimmy. I doubt he would tolerate nicknames. Not proper Mr. Stevenson.

Okay, okay, enough dilly-dallying. Deep breath. Here's what happened.

During the day we were all business. We had meetings all day with very important clients, and I took notes and supplied all the needed documents and papers we've spent the past month pulling together. I was very professional in my new suit, and the sexy lingerie underneath just added to my confidence.

The meetings were interminable, but at the end of the day, we went our separate ways. Mr. Stevenson and I checked into the Hallmark, which was quite a step up from the Howard Johnson, let me tell you. We had adjoining rooms with a connecting door.

He had the key.

When Mr. Stevenson suggested a drink before dinner to celebrate the conclusion of a very successful deal, I accepted, feeling as if I were going on a date, as excited and nervous as a cat. I left off my suit jacket, appearing in only my silk blouse and skirt. Mr. Stevenson had the same basic idea, as he'd removed his jacket and tie. I ordered a Tom Collins. Mr. Stevenson had a martini.

We made small talk and he complimented me on my work during the meetings, which made me feel all warm and happy. He ordered us a second round, though I was already feeling no pain. Then he put his hand on mine and said quietly, "Are you ready, Olivia? Ready for the next step between us?"

Ready?

Could a person be ready for this?

I wasn't entirely sure what I was to be ready for, though I was pretty sure it involved the further breaking of my marriage vows. But, no doubt aided by the gin, a part of my brain said, "What the hell? You've come this far. In for a penny, in for a pound."

"I think so, Mr. Stevenson," I ventured, my heart fluttering wildly.

Another man at that point would surely have said, "Please, call me James." But he didn't.

Instead, he said, "Tonight I want to take you beyond limits you may think you have. I want to know that you are willing. And if you're not, believe me, that's fine. We will continue as we have been at work, and no hard feelings."

He paused and looked at me. I didn't say anything, but I was all ears.

"I want to find out if our connection goes beyond the rather tame games we've been playing at work. I want to test the sincerity of your submission." Again he paused. "Well? What do you say, Olivia? Do you accept?"

My tongue was loosened by alcohol and by the fact we were no longer in an office, but more like on a date. "I'm not really sure what you're talking about," I replied, though I had some idea it involved getting naked. "You talk in circles." I finished off my second drink and set the glass down rather too hard. "Just what is it you want? What do you expect from me?"

"It's a fair question," he said, flashing a rare smile. "And a direct one. So, I'll be direct with you." He leaned forward across the small table and goosebumps rose on my skin. "You excite me. You're beautiful and sexy. More than that, I've come to value our relationship, aside from our professional one, of course, which is also highly satisfactory. What I'm trying to say is that I want you, Olivia."

"Oh," I whispered, stunned by his declaration.

"Not just for a romp in the sheets," he continued. "I believe you and I are destined for more than that. I have been seeking a kindred connection for some time now, and I believe I have found it with you. I hope you'll find the courage to explore it further with me. If you accept, you will have the chance to submit in the way I think you long for, and I will have the chance to dominate, in a sensual sense, a woman who was born to it."

"Oh," I repeated like an idiot, any coherent response blasted from my brain by his astonishing words. Kindred connection. It sounded so romantic. Not *just* a romp in the sheets. So romping was to be a part of it? Well, of course. What had I expected?

He was watching me, his face vulnerable for the first time in memory, stark with a need that both startled and moved me.

"Yes," I finally found the wherewithal to whisper. "I accept."

He called over the waitress and told her his room number and to put the drinks on his tab. "We can go first for dinner or…" He let the sentence hang.

"I don't think I could eat a bite," I replied truthfully. My stomach was in knots of nervous anticipation.

"Room service later," he agreed.

We rode up in the large, quiet elevator to our floor. He unlocked my door and said, "I want you to get ready for me, Olivia. Please know I have no plan to destroy your family or make any demands on you outside of the time we have together."

I appreciated what he was saying, and I understood this wasn't just about me. He has as much to lose as I do. I nodded.

He opened my door and said quietly, "You will undress to bra, panties and stockings. You may remove your shoes. You will kneel on the carpet, head touching the ground, arms extended in front of you, ass in the air. You will wait quietly in that position. You will not speak or move when you hear me enter. I expect absolute obedience. Do you understand?"

I was dizzy from the drinks, but it was more than that. His words sent me reeling. Was the man insane? My usual voices piped up in my head, trying to pretend outrage, but I knew at the same time I was going to do it. His words resonated with that dark, secret part of me I'm only just coming to terms with.

"Yes, Sir," I managed to whisper.

He shut my door, leaving me alone in the lovely room. The bed had been turned down and there was a small chocolate wrapped in gold foil set in the center of a plump pillow.

I used the toilet and removed my clothing as directed. I glanced in the mirror, brushed my hair, applied fresh lipstick and returned to the bedroom. I took a big breath, asked myself out loud what the heck I was doing.

It's hard to describe the feelings that coursed through me as I waited on my knees, head down, bottom up, for Mr. Stevenson to enter the room. I waited for an hour or more in that position. No, it only felt like that. In fact it was more like five minutes, but that was plenty long enough.

I tensed when I heard the sound of the deadbolt turning in the door between our rooms. He entered quietly, his steps muffled by the soft, thick carpet. His bare feet appeared in my line of vision. His warm hand skimmed my back and my heart did a somersault in my chest. I started to rise but he said, "Don't move."

My heart was thumping so loudly I'm sure he could hear it too. He crouched, his mouth close to my ear. "Olivia, for the rest of the night you belong to me. I will use you in whatever way I see fit, in any way I choose. If you accept these terms, stay kneeling as you are. If you have changed your mind, get up now and I'll go back to my room. Dress and we'll have dinner downstairs and that will be that. We can still go on as before in the office. Please understand, this is not an ultimatum. I don't want you unless you're ready to give yourself to me."

I stayed down, though now my heart seemed to have lodged itself in my throat. After about five interminable seconds, he placed his hands on my shoulders. I allowed him to pull me upright. I thought I might faint, but at the same time I was electrified with excitement.

We were standing now face-to-face. Looking down at me with those crystalline eyes, he wrapped me in his strong arms and bent down, kissing me with the ardency of a lover. His hands were roaming over my back and bottom, and I responded, pressing into him, this time bringing my own arms around him as I'd fantasized so many times before.

After a few moments, he pulled away and murmured, "For tonight, you are to call me Master." He looked past my eyes into my soul. "And to me you will be only slave. No names tonight, not even surnames. Do you understand?"

Writing this now, it sounds kind of silly, like something out of some trashy novel, but at the time, it was anything but. I don't know how to convey it, but everything about the experience seems heightened somehow in my memory. Colors were brighter, sensations more vivid. I felt so alive, as if the rest of my life was cast in shadowy grays.

He took off my underthings, though I don't specifically recall him doing it. He was kissing me the whole time. He was still in his trousers and undershirt, which didn't seem quite fair. "Have you ever been whipped, slave?" he said in a calm voice, as if this were a perfectly reasonable question.

My mouth fell open in shock.

"No, of course not," he answered for me. "And now in your mind, you're imagining some kind of Marquis de Sade torture. But it isn't. It isn't when it's done right, as a loving act. I'm going to show you, slave. I'm going to introduce you to something you've never dreamed about. Now lie down on your stomach and relax." He pointed to the bed. "I'll be right back."

In a kind of paralyzed shock, I lay on the bed as directed, my mind curiously blank.

When he returned, he had removed his shirt. He had nice curling chest hair over a firmly muscled chest. I was distracted by what he was holding—a black whip with dozens of leather throws hanging from a long handle.

I gasped and sat up, clutching myself protectively.

He was next to me in a flash. Sitting on the bed, he gently pushed me back down to mattress. "This will only happen at your pace. You will call the shots. You will ask me for more when you're ready. Until then, let me show you how sensual a flogger can be." His touch was gentle, his words soothing, so at odds with the stern Mr. Stevenson from the office. And yet, not really. It was just another facet, I suppose, of a complicated man.

I closed my eyes, enjoying the feel of the soft, expensive sheets beneath my naked body, and his hands moving in slow, sensual circles over my shoulders, back and bottom. Eventually, I realized it was no longer his hands on my flesh, but the soft tresses of the flogger gliding up and down my back, bottom and thighs. And he was right—it was soft, sensual—lovely, really.

He continued to run the leather up and down my body until my flesh was tingling, a warm, throbbing ache between my legs. As he'd predicted, I began to wonder what it would feel like if he were to raise the whip and let the tresses fall harder against my skin.

"Please, Master," I ventured, feeling both ridiculous and deeply excited. "Perhaps a little harder?"

"Yes, slave," he replied. "As you wish." The leather snapped in a flurry against my ass. It stung, though not too much. At the same time, it ignited something deep in my core. He continued like this for several minutes, slowly increasing the intensity of the strokes.

I drifted in the sensations, at once utterly relaxed and wildly alive.

"Spread your legs, slave," he eventually commanded.

Too aroused to be shocked, I did as he said.

He placed his hand there and, to my deep embarrassment, murmured, "You're soaking wet, slave. You need this. You need more than I'm giving you now, don't you?"

Though I still don't understand it, he was right. I needed more. I nodded.

"Then ask for it, slave. Ask me to whip you harder. To make you wetter." His fingers swirled over my sex and one pressed its way into me. I actually groaned aloud with lust.

"Please, Master," I managed, the honorific sliding out of my mouth like it had always been under my tongue. "Whip me harder." I tensed, suddenly afraid of what I'd asked for.

The flogger came down with a slapping sound, and this time it really stung. With a gasp, I jerked under the lash. He did it again. And again.

Here's the weird thing, the thing I've been wrestling with. The whipping stung like a dozen bees buzzing over my body, but, while it hurt, I didn't want it to stop. He alternated stroking my sex with his fingers and whipping my back, ass and thighs with his flogger until it all got mixed up somehow—the pleasure and pain intertwining into something I have no words for.

"Yes," he breathed, continuing to whip me harder and harder, all the while stroking my sex until I was wriggling around, my skin on fire, passion making my blood boil. Unaware of what I was doing, I rolled over suddenly, and his flogger struck my breasts, the tips whipping across my right nipple like needles.

I squealed and instinctively covered my breasts with my hands, the pleasure receding.

He dropped the flogger and lowered his mouth to my stinging nipple. As his tongue moved over it, the sting was erased, though the fire in my belly only intensified. Utterly shameless, I reached for him and pulled him down on top of me, seeking his mouth, those lips, with mine.

He held me close as he kissed me. I could feel his erection beneath his trousers. "I want you," he breathed in my ear. "I must have you."

"Yes," I groaned in reply. "Please."

He lifted himself from me long enough to pull off the rest of his clothing. He had one of those condom things, and I suppose I was glad he'd thought of that, though somehow it made what we were doing less of a fantasy, more of a cold reality—we were committing adultery, no matter how you sliced it.

When he entered me, I began to convulse. For a second, I was afraid I was having a seizure, but as he began to move inside me, I realized I was having an orgasm, and then my mind shut off as he made love to me for what seemed like hours.

I woke sometime in the middle of the night. I was alone in my bed, Mr. Stevenson long gone. I lay there awake for a long time, reliving the stunning events of the evening, both shocked and thrilled at what had taken place between us.

Now we're back at the office, once again Mr. Stevenson and Olivia, boss and secretary, with no mention of what happened, and no idea of when it might happen again.

I'll admit it here. I'm not sorry it happened. In fact, I can't stop thinking about it. I want what he offers. I want more than he's offered so far. Now the question is, how am I going to get it?

~*~

"Wow," Tess murmured, letting Olivia's journal slide from her hands. She turned to Ryan in the bed. "He whipped her. He actually whipped Olivia. I can't even imagine it."

"Can't you, Tess?"

Tess swallowed hard. She'd had a full-blown daydream after reading *Charlotte's Awakening*, one she had yet to share with Ryan. In the fantasy, Tess was standing in a room, her arms raised high overhead, her wrists bound in thick rope. Her ankles were also bound, forcing her to stand with legs far apart. She was naked, her skin gleaming with sweat.

Ryan stood behind her. Though he didn't say a word, she could sense his power, both sensual and dangerous. The only sound in the room was her own rapid breathing. Though she couldn't see him, somehow she knew he was holding a whip. Not a flogger as Olivia had described, but a long, single tail whip, coiled like a snake in his hand, ready to strike.

Ryan was watching her now. He repeated the question. "Can't you imagine that whipping, Tess?"

"Yes," she admitted softly. Why not tell him the truth? She could trust him. "I actually had this daydream after reading the novel you gave me."

"Tell me."

She described the fantasy, though putting the underlying feelings into words was harder than just describing the scenario. "It seemed so real. Like every nerve in my body was poised and waiting for the cut of the lash against my skin."

"Did you want it? Do you want to experience that for yourself?"

"I-I don't know. I do. And I don't. If that even makes sense."

"You're afraid but curious."

"Yes," Tess agreed, not sure which feeling was stronger.

Ryan leaned over her, kissing her eyelids shut. Speaking in a soft, seductive voice, he murmured, "I love the fantasy you've created, Tess. I can totally imagine it. You, tied and bound, helpless really, the thick rope snug around your wrists and ankles. There's no way out. You're completely at your Master's mercy. He possesses you at that moment, in every sense of the word."

Tess shivered at Ryan's words.

He stroked her right nipple and captured it between thumb and forefinger, squeezing lightly at first, and then harder. "In the fantasy, you're turned on but scared. There's no one there to set you free, no one but the Master to hear your cries." His voice had deepened, his words weaving a sensual spell over her. "You have to take it, Tess. To take the whipping. Your Master is aware of your fear, but also of your need. He leads you slowly, carefully, but inexorably, to that dark, sensual place where pain and pleasure no longer have separate meaning."

"Oh my god," Tess breathed, feeling both hot and cold. "It's like you're inside my head." She turned to him. "Is that what *you* want, Ryan? Would it excite you to whip a woman?"

To whip me.

Ryan's smile was slow and sensual, his eyes glittering with lust. "Yes, Tess. It's what I want. It's what I've always wanted, but I'd never found the right woman. Until now."

Tess drew in a breath, her heart pounding. He reached for her, pulling her closer. As she nestled against him, he said, "Are you ready to go to the next level, Tess? To turn your fantasies into reality?"

Tess thought a while before answering, honestly weighing her conflicting feelings in her mind. "It's weird," she finally said, "because while it really turned me on to read all that stuff in *Charlotte's Awakening*, I don't know if I could handle that kind of intensity in real life. I mean, I'm not into pain. I don't like stubbing my toe. I considered getting a tattoo once, but the thought of the needles made me woozy. Not to mention, I'm a firm believer in equality and women's rights. So why did I get so incredibly turned on when Charlotte was chained and brutally whipped, not only by her lover, but by his butler? Why did I get such a dark thrill when she was raped by the guy's chauffeur and then casually sodomized by her lover?"

Ryan snorted, though his expression was thoughtful. "I totally get what you're saying. Regarding women's rights, there's no conflict. You can be a kickass attorney and completely in charge of your own affairs and decisions, but still choose to submit sexually to your partner. I think that's the crux of it—choice. A consensual, informed and willing exchange of power. True liberation is the freedom to actually be who you are. To be true to yourself, and that doesn't just include women."

"That makes sense," Tess agreed. "I never really thought about it that way, but yeah. I like that."

Ryan nodded. "And regarding erotic pain, stubbing your toe or getting repeatedly poked by a tattoo artist has nothing to do with it. Being a sexual masochist, or a sensual sadist for that matter, is a whole different experience. It's not about inflicting or receiving the pain per se. It's about erotic domination and submission. It's about surrender and trust. It's about sensation, and the incredible rush, both physical and mental, of a true exchange of power."

He stroked her hair, his voice calm, but she could feel the intensity beneath it—his need for her to understand, and the underlying trust that went with it. She fell a little more in love with him, if that was possible.

"I've had a little experience," he went on, "and I've done a lot of reading and research about BDSM, and what I've come to realize is that we're hardwired a particular way, sexually speaking. We may or may not choose to act on those feelings, but I'm dominant and sensually sadistic—it's a part of who I am at my core, just like I believe you're submissive and sexually masochistic. Mainstream acceptance of this kind of sexuality is still relatively new, and certainly not universal. BDSM is still largely misunderstood by most people."

Tess nodded. "I get it. I think I've always had these feelings, but I never dared to act on them. I'm so glad I found Olivia's diaries, even if it's still hard to get my head around the fact she's my grandmother."

She gave a small laugh.

"And I'm glad you shared them with me," Ryan said. "Her journals are like a gateway for us. They've given us permission to explore our own D/s connection, on our own terms. And we're lucky. We don't have to sneak around. We don't have to feel guilty about what we're doing."

She stroked Ryan's smooth chest. "So you're hardwired to be sexually dominant, but you've waited until you're practically thirty to act on it?" she said in a teasing voice, though her heart was beating fast, her mind reeling with the possibilities.

"I guess I was waiting for the right woman," he replied seriously. "Trust is a two-way street, as you know. I feel safe with you—safe to express my true feelings and desires."

Tess warmed at his words. "Thank you," she said softly. "I didn't mean to make light of your feelings. I'm honored to be your safe place, and I feel the same way. It's just so much to take in. To-to admit to *myself*, much less another person, that I want to be tied down, to be controlled, to be…whipped." It was hard even to say the words, but at the same time somehow freeing.

"And yet, for you," Ryan replied, "when you can throw off all the noise from societal expectations and norms and all that other crap, it's the most natural thing in the world, because it's a part of what you are. It's like being gay or left-handed. You can pretend to be hetero, or make yourself learn to write with your right hand, but in the end, you still are what you are. The cool thing—the awesome thing—is when you can get to a place where you not only accept that about yourself, but embrace it—celebrate it."

He pushed her gently onto her back and leaned up beside her to stare down into her eyes. "It's like Olivia's Mr. Stevenson said. You and I have found this rare, kindred connection. We have the chance to discover together where it might take us." He stroked her cheek and then slid his hand below her jawline, his fingers spanning out to grip her lightly by the throat.

His touch sent a shiver of both fear and lust hurtling through her frame. She stared up into his eyes, mesmerized by his gaze, his words, and the power implied in his primal grip. "This is the opportunity we've both been waiting all our lives for. The question is, do we have the courage to seize it?"

Chapter 7

December 4, 1961

Okay, it's been way too long since I wrote in this thing. I realized it when he asked me this morning how my journal is going. He still wants me to write about what I'm feeling, to explore it honestly and without editing my reactions.

"This isn't for my consumption," he reminded me. "It is for yours alone. Your journal is a place to express your feelings without censoring them. Be honest with yourself. That can be harder than you think."

He's right. Sometimes, I find myself wanting to deny my own feelings, or deny that something aroused me. I have to wonder—are there others out there like me? Like him? Is our behavior sick and twisted, or, as Mr. Stevenson calmly assures me, just another facet of our innate sexuality?

Where do I start?

Things between us are definitely more...intimate. No question, we crossed a line at the hotel. I've betrayed my husband in such a final and absolute sense. Though if I'm really honest, I betrayed Frank the first time I let Mr. Stevenson use a ruler, or permitted him to stare at me in that way he has, as if he can see not only through my clothing, but into my very heart and soul.

And yet, at the same time I don't feel as if I've betrayed anyone. I am still the same Livvie at home, taking care of Frank and kids, involved in everyone's lives, behaving as I always do. If anything, guilt has driven me to be even more attentive to my husband. And as long as I keep it ladylike and am not too demanding—I'm coming to realize how ridiculous this is, the limits we put on ourselves and let others put on us—Frank seems happy enough with our sex life.

I am reasonably able to compartmentalize my life, leaving my submissive behaviors and Mr. Stevenson's influence here at the office when I leave. It's best to keep what we have just where we have it.

But what is it, exactly, that we have?

Perhaps I'll just write for a while. Describe some of the things we've begun to incorporate into our strange little world here in this office.

My daily routine has changed somewhat. I still come in a half-hour before Mr. Stevenson and remove my girdle and practical underpants, replacing them with a garter belt and pretty panties. I have a dozen pairs now, and I wash them out at the end of the day and leave them discreetly to dry overnight on a rack I brought in for the purpose.

But now, if we aren't expecting any clients, I am to remove my bra as well, but put back my dress or blouse and jacket. Sometimes, he'll take no notice of my state of semi-undress the entire day, but I'm always hyper-aware of it. At first I was mildly scandalized at going without a bra, something I never do, even at home under my housedress. But I rather like the sensation, and the freedom. Several times a day I'll go into the bathroom and reach into my blouse to touch my nipples. They have become "needy"—Mr. Stevenson's term.

He explains that he wants each part of my body to become needy, to experience a constant readiness and desire for his touch, whether it be gentle or harsh.

Yesterday, he came to stand in front of my desk. I was just completing a letter and I finished typing the sentence before looking up at him.

"Unbutton your blouse."

Keeping my eyes on his face, I obediently unbuttoned the top two buttons of my blouse, my heart racing, nipples instantly erect. He nodded, indicating I should continue. Even though he's seen me completely naked, I still feel shy displaying myself like that. I love to obey him, however. It satisfies something deep in my soul. I undid all the buttons, pulling the blouse from my skirt to get at the bottom ones.

Mr. Stevenson placed his hand inside the open blouse and cupped my left breast. I'm sure he could feel the thudding of my heart. Using his thumb and forefinger, he rolled my nipple, gently at first, then with more pressure.

Heat rushed into my face as he fondled me. It's so annoying the way I constantly blush. I wish I could control that, but Mr. Stevenson say he enjoys eliciting that response in me. I still hate it.

Anyway, he drew his hand away and my other breast felt "needy"—it wanted to be touched and teased too. He pulled the blouse from my shoulders, completely exposing me. I had to grip the desk to resist my impulse to cover myself. At the same time, I was hot and wet between my legs.

"What do you want, Olivia?"

I didn't answer right away, not sure what to say—how much to admit.

"I asked you a question, Olivia," he said, his voice growing stern. "You will answer me."

"I-I want you to touch my other breast," I admitted.

His smile was cruel, his eyes glittering like chips of blue ice as he reached for my other nipple and caught it in a sudden, painful twist.

It hurt.

But along with the pain came the same dark, urgent thrill I'd experienced when he'd flogged me that night at the hotel. I don't understand myself—how I can both hate and crave the pain, but Mr. Stevenson says that's okay. He says he will understand for both of us. All I have to do is accept it.

After teasing and twisting my nipples until I was a panting wreck, he said casually, "You know, a good legal secretary should always exhibit excellent powers of concentration. Let's see how well you can concentrate, Olivia, while being distracted." He lifted a sheet of paper from a file on my desk. "Have you prepared these briefs yet?"

"No, Sir." I looked down. My nipples were poking from my breasts like hard red cherries.

"You will begin with this one." He set the page on my typewriter. "Type up the comments I've made in the margins. Focus completely on your task, no matter what I do to you. Do you understand?"

I nodded, biting back a yelp of nervous excitement. I'll admit it, I love this kind of game, and I was hot to trot.

Then he added, "I'm going to inspect your work, Olivia. For each error I find, I will punish you. Is that clear?"

"Yes, Sir," I said, some of my excitement dampened by his threat. I was determined to produce a flawless product. Taking a fresh sheet of bond from the drawer, I slid it into my trusty typewriter, trying to act calm and professional, which is hard to do when your blouse is hanging off your shoulders, your bare breasts on full display.

Mr. Stevenson moved to stand behind me. At first, I had no problem focusing, but then he placed his hands on my shoulders. He pushed the blouse farther down so it hampered my arms as I tried to type.

I thought about just wriggling out of it so I could type more effectively, but he hadn't said anything about removing the blouse, so I just gamely continued typing. Meanwhile his hands moved from my shoulders to my breasts. Still behind me, he took each nipple between thumb and forefinger and began to roll them, sending waves of pleasure, and sometimes of pain when he tweaked too hard, through my body.

The more aroused I got, the harder it was to focus. When he lowered his head to nuzzle my neck, my hands fell away from the typewriter and I sighed with pleasure.

He pulled away and snapped, "Olivia, pay attention to what you're doing. You forget yourself."

My eyes, which had fluttered shut of their own accord, popped open as I put my hands back into position on the keyboard. Just as I was finding my place again, he gripped my nipples, twisting them so hard I yelped, my fingers fumbling as they smacked the wrong keys.

"Focus," he commanded in a hard voice.

I tried to obey, and I did manage a few more lines, but I was so aroused and confused by the sensations of heat and desire deep in my belly, juxtaposed with the twisting pain at my nipples, that I barely knew what I was doing.

I couldn't seem to catch my breath, and finally I gave up trying to type. He pulled my head back and kissed me hard on the mouth. If he'd ordered me to strip and lie down on the carpet, I would have done it.

But he didn't. We only ever did "it" the one time. I have no idea if we'll ever do "it" again.

I wonder about that. We play games that are increasingly sexual in nature, but he always stops the action before things go too far. That time was no exception. Mr. Stevenson kissed me a while and it was heavenly, but then abruptly, he pulled away and stood up, still completely composed, though his eyes were glittering.

"You may button your blouse," he said without a trace of emotion. "Then come to my office. Bring your typing."

Well, of course there were typos galore, but whose fault was that?

I stood in front of his desk, my blouse untucked, lipstick smeared across my face, my hair a mess. My bottom was twitching in anticipation of the ruler I was sure was coming.

But instead of ordering me to bend over to take my well-earned punishment, he said, "Olivia, I've sensed that you are coming to, ah, enjoy our little punishment sessions. Which really isn't surprising, as I had you pegged as a masochist from your first week here."

I blushed, as usual, but also as usual, he was right on the money.

"Today we're going to try something different. The punishment will be more overtly sexual in nature, but I think you are at the point where you can handle it, slave."

Don't think I didn't notice him calling me that. He hadn't called me that since the hotel, and I hadn't called him Master either.

He went on. "Today you have a choice. You may either fellate me, or use your own hand to bring yourself to orgasm in front of me."

You could have knocked me over with a feather. Fellate him? Who even uses words like that? But beyond the words is the deed. Though I'm perfectly aware there are women who do this for their husbands, I'm certainly not one of them. It's not that I'm horrified by the idea, but Frank would never tolerate it, if it even occurred to him, which I doubt it has.

Of course, masturbating in front of Mr. Stevenson wasn't a whole lot better of an option, but it was at least the lesser of the two evils. The thing is, I've touched myself before, but it's never amounted to much—certainly not an orgasm like the kind Mr. Stevenson has given me. It's more like scratching an itch.

At first, I just stood there staring at him. He stared back, his gaze making me shift and shuffle like a nervous kid.

"Well, slave?"

"I really couldn't—" I hedged, but he interrupted me.

"Of course you can. You can do what I tell you, because you belong to me. Did you forget that so quickly?"

His words were like a warm, heavy blanket settling over me. It's hard to explain, but when he talks like that, it both calms and thrills me all at once. "I-I'll touch myself," I managed haltingly.

"Speak up. Don't mumble, slave."

I cleared my throat, my cheeks burning. "I'll touch myself, Master." I felt both ridiculous and somehow empowered by calling him that.

A smile of approval lifted his lips. "Very good, slave. I'm delighted you have the courage to proceed." He gestured toward the couch.

As I sat, he said, "You may leave on the skirt. I want you to hike it up and remove your panties."

It was humiliating to sit like that, my skirt bunched up around my waist, my privates exposed, and it only got worse when he ordered, "Scoot to the edge of the couch and spread your legs wide. I want to watch."

I was so embarrassed, I couldn't meet his gaze, but I did as he said. Closing my eyes, I rubbed myself vigorously, nervous as a cat.

After a few minutes, he said, "Slow down and ease up a bit. Take your time. I want you to lick your fingers and then lean back while you're touching yourself. I want you to relax."

Though I kept my eyes shut, I could feel his gaze moving over me. I hoped I didn't look too ridiculous, splayed out, my hand buried between my legs. Frank would have been horrified, but Mr. Stevenson said, "You look so beautiful like that, Olivia. So sexy."

A rush of happiness and warmth flooded through me at his words, and I actually began to relax, at least a little. It started to feel good, and I sighed with pleasure, though I remained keenly aware of his eyes on me. Knowing he was watching me, while embarrassing, was also what made it so exciting. The experience was nothing like the occasional fumbling I'd done alone from time to time.

"Olivia. You are my slut. You bare yourself for me and make yourself come for me because you belong to me. Right now, I could call in one of our clients to join me here, if I wanted to. It's my prerogative. I might say to him, 'This is Olivia, my personal slave. She does precisely what I tell her to do.' And you know what you would do in that situation? You would stay right where you are and keep rubbing yourself like the slut you are, until I told you to stop."

If any man had spoken to me to me like that in any other context, I would have slapped him into tomorrow, but with Mr. Stevenson it was…perfect. If I'd been processing his words with my brain, I would have been outraged, but my brain had vacated the premises. His words entwined with my fingers, as if they were touching me directly. I began to get dizzy, and my breath was ragged as I stroked and rubbed myself with increasing abandon.

"Come for me, Olivia," he said softly.

And, heaven help me, I did.

This was way more than just scratching an itch. I forgot to be embarrassed. I was barely aware of Mr. Stevenson for that brief, suspended moment in time. I was just sensation. Pure, raw ecstasy.

When I came back to myself Mr. Stevenson was kneeling right in front of me, his hands on either of my bare thighs. "You never cease to surprise me, Olivia," he said, smiling broadly. Gently, he brought my thighs together and smoothed my hair from my forehead. It was a lover's touch.

I was completely spent. It was like I had run a race. I also felt wonderful—euphoric. That's the word. It was better than…than ice cream!

~*~

Tess laughed aloud. She could almost hear her grandmother saying those words—she had loved ice cream—especially mint chocolate chip—above all things. She glanced at Ryan, but he wasn't smiling.

His expression was intense, his green eyes hooded with lust. "Would you do that for me, Tess? If I asked it of you, would you spread your legs for me at the office and make yourself come?"

Tess laughed, assuming he must be joking, though a frisson of excitement shot through her at the thought. "Oh, yeah, right," she said lightly. "Which one of us would be accused of sexual harassment when they caught us, huh?"

"Who says we'd be caught?"

~*~

The next day at six o'clock, Ryan stuck his head into Tess's office. While most of the support staff had gone, many of the attorneys were still hard at work, or milling about in the open areas of the large suite of offices, discussing cases or just shooting the breeze.

Ryan had been waiting all day for this. "Hey there," he said softly.

Tess looked up from her laptop, distractedly at first, and then with a sudden, sunny smile that shot like an arrow directly through Ryan's heart. She wore a button-down silk blouse, her suit jacket hung over the back of her chair. Tendrils of her dark, shiny hair had escaped her chignon.

He entered her office and closed the door, discreetly pushing the lock button in the doorknob. "Remember what we talked about last night?"

She gave him a blank look, so he elaborated.

"What you're going to do for me today. In your office, as Mr. Stevenson had Olivia do for him?"

"Oh," she said softly, a pretty, pink flush moving over her cheeks. "I-I do remember"—she glanced at the closed door—"but—"

"No buts," Ryan interrupted. "Go sit on the couch. Lift your skirt and take off your panties."

She swallowed visibly, but she got to her feet and walked over to her couch. Her big brown eyes on his, she pushed her panties down her smooth legs and lifted her narrow skirt so her bare bottom rested on the leather upholstery.

"Scoot to the edge," Ryan commanded, consciously recreating the scene that had been enacted so long ago. "Spread your legs and make yourself come for me, Tess. And don't close your eyes. Keep them on my face."

"Yes, Sir," she breathed, her eyes shining, though her hand trembled slightly as she placed it between her legs.

Ryan's cock swelled and hardened as he watched his beautiful lover stroking herself on her office couch, her gaze on his face, her breath coming faster and faster as she neared climax.

Ryan took a seat in one of the chairs in front of her desk, swiveling it so he was facing her. It took all his self-control not to yank off his clothes and fuck her right then and there. He contented himself instead by unbuckling his belt and opening his fly so he could adjust his erect cock.

"Oh, oh, oh," she began to pant, clearly about to come.

Now for the test.

"Stop," Ryan ordered.

She furrowed her brow in obvious frustration but, he was pleased to note, dropped her hand. She glanced toward the office door. "Is someone coming?" she whispered anxiously.

"No. I just don't want you to come yet. You'll wait for permission."

Tess took a deep, shuddery breath. He could almost see the fight taking place inside her. She'd been so close to climax, but she also craved the submissive relinquishment of erotic control. After a moment, she nodded slowly.

"Stand up," he ordered.

She rose to her feet and started to pull her skirt, which was bunched up around her hips, down over her thighs.

"No," Ryan said. "Leave it hiked up like that. I like seeing you exposed." He pointed to the carpet. "Get on your knees and crawl over to me." He reached into his underwear and pulled his erect shaft free, his intention obvious.

Would she do it?

Ryan's heart skipped a beat as Tess dropped to her knees and began to crawl toward him, the very picture of erotic submission. She knelt up in front of him, her lush lips parted, her cheeks flushed, her eyes bright with lust.

She flashed an impish, decidedly un-submissive grin toward Ryan, who, despite his efforts to maintain a stern Master persona, grinned back. He glanced over her head at the office door. This wasn't the smartest thing he'd ever done, having his lover suck him off at the office, but he was no longer thinking with his big head.

Tess cupped his balls through the thin fabric of his underwear as she lowered her head over his exposed shaft. He sighed with pleasure as she licked around the crown and then closed her lips over his cock. He placed his hand lightly on her head, guiding himself into her mouth.

He groaned as she suckled and teased him. He let her work her magic for a minute or two more. The pleasure was nearly unbearable, but he didn't want to come. Not yet. He had another idea. He pushed her gently but firmly away.

She looked up at him in surprise. "What's the matter?"

"Nothing. But I have something else in mind." He got to his feet. "Crawl after me into your bathroom." He couldn't quite believe she was actually on her hands and knees behind him. Her submission was thrilling to him, and he recognized what an extraordinary gift it was.

Once they were inside Tess's small, private bathroom, Ryan removed his tie. "Kneel up and put your hands behind your back."

Tess did as he said. He could feel her excitement, which radiated from her like an erotic force field as he bound her wrists together. Returning to stand in front of her, he pulled his trousers and underwear to his knees. Reaching down he unbuttoned her blouse, pulling it free of her skirt to reveal her lace-covered breasts.

His cock throbbing, he crouched in front of her and put his hand between her legs. "Are you wet for me, sub girl?" he asked as he pressed a finger into her tight heat. He laughed softly. "Yes, you are. Hot and wet for your Master, as you should be."

She moaned as he stroked her, and though she was blushing, her nipples were fully erect, her breathing ragged.

Dominant power and lust blended into something dark and potent inside Ryan. For the first time in his sex life, he felt right in his skin and just where he needed to be. He had found his sub girl at last.

Pulling his hand from her willing body, he got to his feet and leaned down to take her face in his hands. "I'm going to fuck your mouth with my cock. You're going to submit with grace and take what I give you. Is that understood?"

"Yes, Sir." She stared up at him with such devotion it nearly took his breath away.

Ryan guided his aching shaft into her pretty, open mouth. As the head of his cock touched her soft palate, she gagged a little and tried to pull back.

He held her fast as he admonished gently, "Don't resist me, Tess. Open yourself to me. Give yourself over to my rhythm. Surrender to me."

She gave a slight nod, the only possible response with his cock down her throat, and let her eyes flutter closed.

His hands on either side of her head, Ryan guided himself slowly in and out of her mouth until she was taking his whole shaft without gagging. He began to thrust faster, his excitement building, his balls aching. She looked so fucking hot like that, her blouse open, her skirt hiked up to her hips, her hands tied behind her back, his hard cock deep in her throat.

Unable to hold on another second, Ryan whipped his cock from her mouth and fell to the ground beside her. He pushed her to her side so her back was to him, her arms still bound together. He pulled at the loose knot to release the tie, and spooned her with his body, using one hand to guide his cock between her ass cheeks.

He nudged the head against her hot, wet cunt, and then pushed inside. They groaned together, the sound primal and filled with animal need. Reaching around her body, he cupped her cunt and stroked the hard nubbin of her clit.

"Now, Tess," he urged. "I want you to come for me." He rubbed her clit as he thrust inside her.

Within a minute, Tess began to moan loudly, shuddering and gasping in climax.

Ryan clamped his hand over her mouth. With a laugh, he said breathlessly, "Hush, someone will hear you, baby." Then his body took over, and he came hard inside her, one hand still over her mouth, the other buried between her legs.

He continued to stroke her pussy, pulling several more shuddering, sweet climaxes from her before finally letting his hands fall away.

"Oh, my god," she sighed when she could catch her breath. "I've died and gone to heaven."

Ryan laughed softly and pulled her closer. Nuzzling her ear, he said, "But here's the real question. Was it better than ice cream?"

Chapter 8

December 12, 1961

I've been moping around for a few days at work. It's been too long since Mr. Stevenson used the ruler. As odd as it is to even write these words, I miss the sting, the sexual humiliation, the erotic power of the interaction. I feel so alive when I'm being punished. I guess that isn't really much of a punishment, is it?

Lately I've been taking matters into my own hands again. I purposely left a sentence out of a letter yesterday. This morning I sloshed his coffee. This afternoon I forgot to bring in a key file.

The one thing I didn't do, didn't dare to do, was come out and ask for it. Admit aloud to him that I was craving the sweet heat of that ruler on my bottom. Or, let's be totally honest here, Livvie—I can't stop thinking about the flogger. The way the leather smacked down across my flesh—how it heated me up from the inside out.

Am I sick? Am I wicked?

Mr. Stevenson assures me this is all perfectly natural, and I want to believe him. Submission, he says, freely given and lovingly taken, is the ultimate sensual expression. What evil or harm can there be in a consensual exchange of power? And when he says it, it makes sense.

But it's a lonely business, this secret submission to my boss. I should be sharing my discovery with my husband. Obviously, that's not possible, ever, on any level. Even if I left out what I'm doing at work, even if I just tried to add more "spice" into our sex life, Frank would be confused and horrified. He would never understand, not in a million years. Not that I blame him. He has no frame of reference.

So. I just have to keep these two worlds separate.

Back to Mr. Stevenson, he *finally* called me to account after one coffee slosh too many. "Olivia," he said in that dangerous, sexy way he has when I'm in trouble.

Biting back a squeal of excitement, I entered his office, trying to look calm, my face a mask of innocence, though my panties were already damp with expectation. "Yes, Sir?"

But instead of ordering me to lift my skirt and bend over the desk or go stand in the corner, he said, "We need to talk. Please sit down."

Was this a new game? What were the rules? I took a seat in front of his desk, curious.

He regarded me for a long while, looking into me in that way he has that makes me feel completely naked—body and soul. "Olivia," he finally said. "I know what you're doing. And I even understand why you're doing it. You have come to crave the very punishments that are designed to prevent you from making the careless mistakes that you are now making on purpose. Am I correct?"

I started to deny it, even though it was true, but he cut me off.

"Please. If you're going to lie and pretend not to understand, save us both time and go back to your desk. I want you to be honest, my dear. And to tell you the truth, I am not displeased that you have come to long for the pain and erotic humiliation that you now appreciate can deeply intensify any erotic interaction."

Yes. He really talks like that.

He leaned forward, his expression earnest, even vulnerable. "I think it's time we dispense with these little games, because that's really what they are." He smiled a little as he added, "We do actually have a law practice to run, and I hate to think you're making errors just to satisfy your lust."

I ducked my head, feeling like a fool. The man understands me sometimes better than I do myself.

His voice grew gentle. "Though we haven't talked about it, what we shared that night at the hotel was unique. I will admit to you that I've pulled back some because I was afraid of the intensity of our—of my—feelings. The very nature of a relationship like ours can be so intense that sometimes one can confuse the sensual desire and need to submit or dominate with actual love."

I looked up at this. Was he saying he was in love with me? Or that he didn't dare to fall in love with me? Did he think I was in love with him?

"We're both married," I blurted. "We can't possibly be in love with each other." Even as I said the disingenuous words, I knew how ridiculous it sounded.

But he looked relieved. "No, of course not," he agreed. "We have lives outside of this office. I like to think of this as our private sanctuary. We do share a kind of love, but it isn't something either of us can afford to actualize in any deeper sense. Any permanent sense. That is, uh, I mean, uh…"

Color began to creep up his face. Mr. Stevenson actually seemed to be at a loss for words—a definite first.

Of course I knew what he was trying to say. I took pity on the poor man and spelled it out for him. "You mean you don't want me to get the wrong idea and think we're having a love affair that's going to lead to us ditching our spouses and running off together."

"Well, uh," he mumbled.

I barreled on. "Well, don't you worry, Mr. Stevenson. We're on the same page. I've got three kids who need their daddy, and despite what we have here, whatever that is, I love my husband."

He looked so relieved it was almost comical. "Then we do understand one another," he said, regaining his usual poise. "Which is excellent, as the new phase of your training may make you particularly vulnerable, and I would never want to take advantage of that."

The new phase of my training! Well, and about time, too.

"Going forward," he continued, "I'll still punish you if I feel it necessary, but you're ready to move to a new level of submission. I'm going to teach you the pleasure of pain."

The pleasure of pain.

The words still echo in my head.

My brain instantly tried to tell me that sentence didn't compute, and that pain by definition is not pleasurable, but my body and soul quietly smiled, opening themselves to his words and his promise.

Later: I keep going to the bathroom to look at my bottom. I know I should be horrified, but I'm actually thrilled at the delicate bruises left from the spanking. I'll need to be careful when getting in and out of the shower if Frank's in the bathroom, though I guess I could always say I took a tumble.

You'd think a spanking wouldn't hurt as much as flogging with an actual whip, but you'd be wrong. When it first started, I certainly didn't appreciate the "pleasure" of the pain. It just plain hurt.

After our little talk, Mr. Stevenson got to his feet and went over to his couch. He directed me to approach him and ordered me to remove not only my skirt, but my panties, too.

I took off my skirt and the pink satin panties I'd chosen for that day and laid them neatly on the back of a chair. I stood before him, my hands covering my privates, blushing like a fool.

"Hands at your sides," he directed. "Let me see you. Stand calmly in a relaxed stance. Offer yourself to me. You are my possession to regard and admire."

His possession? Excuse me?

That's what my brain said.

My body whispered, *Yes. Yes, please, Sir.*

Aloud, I said nothing. I just did as I was told.

He raked my bare lower half with a detached expression, though I swear his icy blue eyes were sparkling.

It's hard to describe the potent mixture of arousal and humiliation I experienced as he ogled me as if I were an object. A sex object. But I was damned if I'd let him know how difficult it was for me. I stood my ground, chin raised high, eyes fixed on the middle distance.

Finally, he patted his knees and said, "Come over here. Lie across my lap. I'm going to give you your first proper spanking, slave. I'm going to spank you until I'm ready to stop. You can cry out as much as you wish, but I don't want you wriggling away or telling me to stop. Those are not your prerogatives. *I* will decide when you've had enough."

He waited as I draped myself somewhat awkwardly over his knees, my cheek resting against the couch cushions. My heart was pounding like a drum in my chest.

I had wanted this.

Hadn't I?

Be careful what you wish for…

He placed his palm on my lower back. His touch made me jump at first, but as he stroked and soothed me, I began to calm down.

"This will be your first test in this new phase of submission. The spanking will hurt, make no mistake, but I want you to focus on the pleasure of the pain. I want you to experience it as sensation. Erotic sensation. And know that you will be pleasing your Master, because this is what I want for you. I want to hurt you, but in a way that gives us both pleasure."

Sounds like gobbledygook, right? Utter nonsense.

No. Only to the uninitiated. To me, it made perfect sense.

Beneath his wool trousers, his erection bulged against my thigh, which pleased me. He can pretend to be cool as a cucumber, but it turns out he's still a man, after all.

He began lightly at first, patting my bottom more than anything, and then slowly building up the intensity. I was reminded of the flogging, and my skin seemed to remember too. It was tingling with anticipation. I wanted to experience the spanking, though I was also genuinely scared to receive it. What if I made a fool of myself?

Then came the first real smack, his hard palm cracking across my bottom. The sound of flesh on flesh resounded in the room, along with the sharp sting.

I yelped.

He placed his other hand on the back of my neck to keep me still.

You can handle this, I told myself. *You can do it*. And at first, I could. But after twenty or so swats, it was really stinging. My poor bottom was on fire. I began to whimper, but when I brought my hands instinctively back to protect myself, he slapped them away.

It wasn't long before I forgot all about being a good, obedient slave girl. I had thought I understood about pain easing into erotic pleasure, but this just plain hurt! I was wriggling around, crying real tears now, but on and on it went. I begged him to let me up, to stop, but he ignored me.

"Take it, slave," he admonished in a husky voice. "It's what you need. It's what you were born for."

Then the strangest thing happened. Somehow, those words—*it's what you were born for*—zapped my panic away. I was able to catch my breath, and I became more aware of the heat building in my sex, mingling in a powerful way with the pain. I began to perceive it differently—not as something to be avoided at all costs, but to receive, to embrace.

Maybe it was just that my perception had changed, but then, isn't perception everything?

All I know is, the pain was no longer something to be avoided. It had shifted somehow. Not to pleasure precisely, but to something more than that. Some kind of blend that was stronger than either pleasure or pain alone. *This* was what he was talking about.

I was no longer struggling or whimpering. I felt relaxed, almost as if I were in some kind of trance. I could still feel his hand crashing down against my bottom, but I no longer wanted him to stop. I loved what he was doing.

I craved it.

Longed for it.

Needed it.

When his hand slipped between my legs, I spread my thighs without a trace of self-consciousness and moaned aloud, giving myself over to his skilled fingers.

I can't describe precisely what happened. Words fail.

I just know I wanted what he was doing, and I didn't want it to stop. His use of the term "slave" is more apt than he knows.

As I write this, I realize I am afraid.

Where is this going? How long can it continue?

~*~

One day several weeks into their relationship, Ryan invited Tess to stay the night at his place. His roommate, Peter, was out of town, and they'd finally have the place to themselves. Tess had yet to meet Peter and his girlfriend, Amy. Trying to find a time when the four of them, all with busy work schedules, could get together, had been like trying to herd cats. She was kind of glad, though, that Ryan and she would have the place to themselves the first time she came over.

Though they'd parked in his garage, he led her around the house to the front door to give her the full effect, which she found oddly touching. She'd half expected a stereotypical bachelor pad, with clothes, empty pizza boxes and beer cans strewn about, but the place was pristine. The high-ceilinged living room was tastefully furnished with soft red leather couches and chairs. The floors were dark hardwood, with handspun rugs placed here and there, and large abstract paintings on the walls.

"Your place is gorgeous," Tess enthused. "Maybe you missed your calling as an interior decorator," she added with a laugh.

"I can't take the credit. My mom helped me with the place. She's an architect. She has a good eye for space and color."

"Maybe I could get her to come to my place next time she's in town," Tess replied, only half joking.

As they entered the kitchen, Tess couldn't help but comment, "Wow, even the kitchen is spotless. You guys are much neater than I am."

Ryan shook his head with a rueful grin. "It won't last. We have a maid who comes in once a week. Yesterday was her day."

As Tess took in the gleaming granite counters and stainless steel appliances, she asked, "Does anyone ever cook in here?"

Ryan grinned. "I heat up takeout in the microwave. Peter's a fantastic cook, though. Sometimes I think I should sell him this place and find somewhere new, since Amy practically lives here when he's in town." He opened a bottle of chardonnay and poured a glass for Tess.

"I have a surprise for you," he said, a sudden mischievous glint in his eye that gave Tess pause.

She took a sip of the cold, crisp wine. "Oh, yeah?" she replied, her stomach swooping with excited anticipation. "Tell me."

"I'll do better than that. I'll show you."

He led her down a hall to what looked like an exercise room, complete with an elliptical, a stationary bicycle and a pile of free weights. "Leave your shoes at the door," he instructed, slipping out of his loafers as she kicked off her sandals. As they entered the room, Tess caught her breath at what she saw in the far corner.

Two thick metal chains hung from large hooks mounted in the ceiling, black leather wrists cuff dangling at the ends. A two-foot metal rod lay on the ground beneath them, a cuff attached at either end. A large, black leather flogger rested in an umbrella stand nearby.

"What in the world?" Tess breathed, awestruck. "Where did you get this stuff?"

"The Stockroom, online. I placed a rush delivery because I can't wait to use it on you."

Tess hugged herself. Ryan had become increasingly dominant in the bedroom, and she thrilled to each new experience as he had introduced light bondage and spanking to their repertoire. But this was a whole other level. "Ryan, I don't know," she said in a small voice, both terrified and thrilled at the prospect of being bound and flogged by her lover.

"That's okay, sweetheart," he said, reaching for the fly of her jeans. "I do." He pulled her jeans down her legs, along with her panties. He lifted the hem of her shirt and pulled it over her head, and then reached back to unclasp her bra.

Tess stood passively as Ryan undressed her. She felt dizzy, but it wasn't the wine.

Ryan pulled off his shirt, revealing his sexy, smooth chest, and Tess's nipples hardened in response. He took her into his arms and gave her a long, lingering kiss. When he let her go, he stared down into her eyes. "It's time, Tess. Time to take you to the next level."

He led her to the corner and crouched beside the metal rod. "This is called a spreader bar. It will help keep you in position while I flog you. Stand over it and spread your legs so I can cuff your ankles."

She obeyed as if in a dream, allowing Ryan to cuff her ankles onto either end of the bar. It felt awkward to have her legs forcibly spread, and it was hard to keep her balance.

Getting to his feet, Ryan lifted her arms one at a time and cuffed her wrists so she was pulled taut, spread eagle and utterly helpless before her Master. Tess's cunt was tingling, her breath already coming fast, though he hadn't yet touched her with the flogger. Could she handle this? What if she freaked out?

Ryan picked up the flogger and held it out so she could see it, drawing his fingers through the long, leather tresses, which were shiny and black, knotted securely at the handle.

He lifted the flogger handle to her lips. "Kiss the whip as proof of your willingness to suffer for me. Kiss the whip that's going to mark you." The words were alarming, and something in his tone was different than before—sharper and darker.

Panic rose suddenly in Tess's gut and she jerked against her restraints. "Ryan, you're scaring me," she gasped.

He lowered the flogger, his expression softening with concern. Bending down, he lightly kissed her lips. "Shh, calm down," he said gently. "You can trust me, Tess. You know I love you and would never harm you. But you also know we're ready for the next level. I want this to be real for both of us. Yes, I am going to flog you, but I'll only give you what you can handle. If it's too much, you can use a safeword. We'll keep it simple. If you feel panicky, and like I'm not listening to you, just say *red light*, okay? I'll stop whatever I'm doing immediately."

"Red light," she repeated, suddenly thrilled that she had her own personal safeword. Yes, she did trust Ryan. And yes, she did want to go to this new level. "Yes. Yes, okay."

Ryan lifted the whip again. "Kiss the whip, Tess."

Charlotte always had to kiss Sir Jonathan's chosen instrument of torture before he used it on her.

Tess brushed the soft leather with her lips.

Ryan reached for the back of her head and drew her into a passionate kiss.

She kissed him back, her entire body on fire with lust and

excitement. She was still scared, but somehow that only added to her excitement.

Finally, Ryan let her head go and took a step back. His cock was clearly outlined in his jeans, and her mouth actually watered at the sight.

The flogger still in his hand, he stepped behind Tess.

She bit her lower lip in nervous anticipation.

The leather whooshed down over her ass, and she jerked reflexively, though the sting was light and easy to tolerate.

He struck her again, this time a little harder—a little surer. "You good?" he asked.

"Yes," she whispered, though her heart was pounding.

He began to smack her ass in a steady beat of leather against flesh, each stroke a little harder than the last. It stung, yes, but it also felt good, or, more accurately, it felt *right*.

Then he struck her hard across both cheeks, the tips curling painfully around her left hip. Tess cried out, trying to twist away, though bound as she was, she couldn't move.

"Breathe," Ryan said. "Flow with it. You're doing great. You were born for this."

Tess drew in a shuddery breath and released it.

"Again," Ryan urged. "Yes. That's better. I'm going to whip you harder now. I want you to accept what I give you. Remember it pleases me to make you suffer in this way."

His words skipped her brain and lodged directly in her bones, which melted with raw lust as she sagged in her chains. *Yes. Yes, yes, yes*, a voice shouted inside her soul, though all she could manage aloud was to pant.

He struck her hard, the leather crashing against her skin in a rippling sound, and she cried out in response. The pain was real, but the dark lust just beneath was real, too. She wanted it. She needed it. She never wanted it to stop.

But when the stinging leather moved its way up Tess's back, she yelped and jerked, pulled from whatever trance she'd been in. "Ow," she yelled, trying in vain to twist away from the lash. Her heart was pounding so hard she could hear it in her ears, and she would have fallen to her knees if she hadn't been held in leather and chains.

"You can do it, Tess. You are doing it," Ryan said, his voice deep and masterful. "You're taking this for me. For your Master." The flogger moved back down to her ass, striking with force.

Tess's mind had stopped processing. She was raw feeling—stinging pain, hot, needy passion, aching sexual desire.

It was too much—too much, and not enough. *Give me more. No, no, stop. Don't stop. Don't ever stop...*

"No," she murmured softly, barely aware she was speaking. "No, no, no, no..." It wasn't a plea, but more of an incantation, which shifted as he continued the flogging to, "Yes, yes, yes, yes..."

Finally, pushed to the very edge of what she could tolerate, Tess begged in a hoarse, ragged voice, "Please. Please fuck me!"

At last Ryan dropped the flogger. He brought his arms around her and pressed his body against her heated flesh. "You are so perfect," he breathed in her ear. He kissed her neck. His erection was hard against her burning ass. "I am so, so proud of you."

Dropping his arms, he appeared in front of her, his green eyes filled with love and fire. "I have to have you. Now."

Crouching, he released her ankles from the spreader bar and then stood, reaching up to undo her wrist cuffs. He caught her as she sagged forward, exhausted but elated. He lifted her into his arms and carried her from the room and down the hall to the bedroom.

He set her gently on the bed. Though the sheets were soft, she winced as her heated flesh made contact. She forgot her discomfort as she watched him strip.

His cock was hard, his eyes flashing with fiery lust. With a primal growl, he fell on top of her, scooping her into his arms and kissing her mouth as his body sought hers.

She was sopping wet and more than ready when he entered her. She wrapped her legs around him, pulling him in deeper. He fucked her hard, each thrust sending a spiral of raw pleasure through her loins.

Tess clung to him, mewling with rising passion. Their bodies were slick with sweat, and Ryan was panting with lust. "You're mine," he whispered fiercely. "You belong to me now, completely."

"Yes," she cried as he lifted her into the arc of a powerful climax. "Yes, Sir. I do."

Chapter 9

December 19, 1961

Mr. Stevenson says it's easy to be obedient when you want what is happening to you. He's right. When he calls my name in that special way, something flips on inside me, and I am instantly his slave girl, ready and eager to do his bidding.

I know it's a game. I mean, it can never be more than that. Yet, sometimes it feels more real—more vivid—than anything else in my life. Sometimes, when I'm just doing something mundane, like cooking at the stove, or playing with the children, or doing needlepoint while Frank sits beside me watching the game, I wonder if they can tell that something has changed inside me. I wonder if I look different somehow. If I've been marked in some secret way by Mr. Stevenson and the life I live in secret away from home.

Mostly I can put it aside. I have to. I am a mother first, of course, and I have a duty to my family. But when I step into the office each morning, something happens. I can almost feel it as if it were a physical thing. Easy-going, innocent Livvie becomes wanton sex slave Olivia.

Once I peel out of the confining girdle, remove my bra, put on my sexy panties and garters, and add a dash of red lipstick, the transformation is complete. When Mr. Stevenson arrives, I bring him his coffee and wait patiently for his orders for the day. Most of them concern the running of the office, but usually something sexy is thrown in.

He might have me bend over his desk so he can inspect some part of me. That makes me blush like crazy, but at the same time, it excites me to the point that I actually tremble. The other day he had me lie back against his desk, my legs spread. He raised the hem of my dress and put his hand in my panties. His fingers were like fire probing against me, turning me to jelly with desire.

Invariably, he brings me to climax when he touches me like this. I've tried doing it myself at home in the bathroom, but I can never even come close to what he does. He's so casual about it, but I can tell he's excited by my squirming and moaning. I used to be so embarrassed when I made involuntary noises, but Mr. Stevenson has assured me it's perfectly natural, and a sign of my submission and surrender. I like that about him—he never judges me, though I guess if he did, that would certainly be a case of the pot calling the kettle black.

I have to admit, as strange as it sounds to my own ears, I love the spankings the best—the ones where he uses his bare hand. Yes, it stings like the dickens, but afterward, I'm so aroused he barely has to touch me before I'm ready to climax. I think he's turned me into a nymphomaniac, but I don't even care. I can say it here where no one but me will ever see—I love every second of it.

The other day his hand was in my panties and I was so close, just about to climax, and the dang phone rang.

Normally, I screen Mr. Stevenson's calls, but he just reached over with his free hand and picked up the receiver. "James Stevenson," he said as calm as you please, as if he didn't have his other hand in his secretary's underpants.

I was embarrassed, to say the least. The sexy spell he'd woven around me vanished, and I felt ridiculous lying among his papers with my legs splayed and dress hiked up.

I started to sit up but he pushed me back down and mouthed the words, "Stay there." Turning his attention back to the call, he said, "And a good morning to you, George. I'm so glad you called. Are you still able to make our meeting?"

As he listened to George's response, he resumed stroking me, and I had to put a hand over my mouth to keep from moaning aloud.

"Excellent," he continued. "Olivia and I will be ready for you. I think you'll be quite pleased. Good, good. See you at eleven. Goodbye."

An 11:00 meeting that involved me? This was the first I was hearing about it. I presumed he was talking to George Vanier, a college friend of his he sometimes met for lunch. Why would he be having something so formal as a meeting that involved his secretary with someone who wasn't even a client? Unless he was going to become a client, and he wanted me there to take notes about whatever the issue might be.

I completely lost my train of thought as Mr. Stevenson pressed my thighs apart and thrust a finger inside me. It wasn't long before I was again on the brink of a climax. Then I heard him say, "Today I'm going to test your obedience, slave girl. Do you wish to obey me?"

"Yes," I gasped, not really grasping the import of what he was saying, totally focused on my own pleasure and release.

"Good girl. Then you may come now."

A few more of those perfect strokes and I was done for. I moaned and pressed against him, shuddering with pleasure.

I lay there a while, sprawled against his desk and trying to recover my composure when Mr. Stevenson said, "George Vanier is aware of our, uh, unique arrangement."

That got my attention.

"Excuse me?" I sat up, flustered, scattering his papers as I did so. I pushed down my dress and wrapped my arms around my torso, the warm pleasure of the orgasm receding fast. "What did you say?"

"I believe you heard me, but I'll elaborate. George is familiar with, and quite interested in, this kind of lifestyle. He shares our predilections, though he's never had the opportunity to experience a relationship based on dominance and submission firsthand."

I had pulled myself somewhat together, but still couldn't quite get a handle on what Mr. Stevenson was saying. "You told him about what we do here?" I squeaked, shocked. "You and me?"

Mr. Stevenson smiled. "Not all the specifics, no. But he does understand that you are not only my secretary, but also my submissive slave girl, and he's very excited that I've invited him for an, uh, demonstration of your obedience."

He moved toward me and placed his hand on my shoulder as he looked into my eyes. "If you refuse, I'll cancel the meeting, of course. If I have overstepped, I apologize. I had believed you were far enough along in your training to be obedient in front of a witness. Do you think you can do that, Olivia? Submit to me in front of another man?"

"No," I said flatly. Was he stark raving mad?

Mr. Stevenson pressed his lips into a thin line of disapproval, and I could see the disappointment in his eyes. I hated to be the cause of those emotions, but what did he honestly expect?

He didn't give up, though. "I'm not asking that you submit in any overtly sexual way to Mr. Vanier. It's more of a demonstration of your obedience to me. I have been so proud of your progress. I suppose I wanted to share the pride with another—to display your submission. I had hoped you would be ready, but again, I apologize if I've overstepped."

I bit my lip, my resolve weakening, my outrage melting away. Mr. Stevenson must think a lot of me to believe I'm to the point in my training that he wants to show me off. While it was risky to let a third party into our secret world, it would be quite exciting and daring to show another person, another man, what we shared. And I actually found it rather touching that Mr. Stevenson seemed so genuinely eager to have a witness. He wasn't ashamed of what we were doing. He was proud of it, and of me.

"I see what you're saying," I finally ventured. "I have to admit I'm kind of nervous about it, but I trust you. If you think it's the right thing, then..."

He smiled broadly, something he rarely does, and I found myself smiling back. "Thank you, Olivia. I appreciate it that you thought it through and didn't just react to your gut." His smile fell away as he added almost wistfully, "Sometimes I wonder what would have happened if we'd met at another time..." He looked away without finishing the sentence, but he didn't have to.

I didn't allow myself to finish it, either, as that line of thought leads nowhere. I put it right out of my head, as I'm sure he did.

While Mr. Vanier wasn't technically a client, I decided to put my bra back on for his impending arrival, though I didn't bother with the slip. I managed reasonably well to focus on my work as the morning ticked by, though I must have looked at the clock a dozen times an hour as the hands edged their way toward our meeting with Mr. Vanier.

A little after eleven, I heard the familiar jingle as someone opened the outer door to our small building. A moment later, the office door opened and in came George Vanier, a slim man of medium height with sandy blond hair. If I didn't know they'd gone to college together, I'd have said he was closer to twenty than thirty, with his round, baby face that I doubt he needs to shave more than once a week.

He took off his fedora and smiled at me. "Good morning, Olivia. Nice to see you again." His voice was surprisingly deep for such a slight man.

I blushed as he hung his hat on one of the pegs by the door, now that I was aware he knew about Mr. Stevenson and me.

Mr. Stevenson appeared at the door of his office. "George, there you are. Glad you could make it." He stepped into the room and the two men shook hands. I was getting antsier by the second. What in the world had I been thinking when I'd agreed to whatever Mr. Stevenson had in mind?

He glanced toward me. "Would you bring us some coffee?"

I was glad for the few minutes it took to get the coffee poured and the tray prepared. "Deep breaths," I kept telling myself. "You can do this. Mr. Stevenson has faith in you. Don't let him down."

I was reasonably calm, at least on the outside, when I brought in the coffee tray. I poured for both men, but not for myself. I was edgy enough without a jolt of caffeine.

They were chatting away about some college buddy who had made good, and barely seemed to notice me, aside from nodding their thanks for the coffee.

I stood there uncertainly for a moment, wondering if I should take my seat on the couch beside Mr. Stevenson, or head back to my desk. "Um," I finally ventured, feeling like an idiot.

They both looked expectantly at me. Mr. Stevenson glanced toward his friend and said wryly, "Patience is not her strong suit." I could have smacked him. Then he continued, "Olivia. Show Mr. Vanier your pretty garters."

I stood frozen in place. I had expected some kind of discussion of parameters, or at least something a little more introductory than that!

I looked from Mr. Stevenson to Mr. Vanier and back again. Mr. Vanier was grinning like a Cheshire cat, all teeth. Mr. Stevenson's face was calm, though I could tell from the slight rise of his eyebrows that he was waiting, a trifle impatiently, for me to obey.

Submitting in front of a witness had seemed rather romantic when I'd been sitting at my desk, anticipating this moment. I had told myself the witnessing was kind of like marriage vows. Where a man and wife exchanged their vows in front of others as a testament to their commitment to one another, Mr. Stevenson and I had the chance to show the unique power of our unusual relationship to another person, and thereby validate it on a level that moved beyond just the two of us.

Trying to remember this lofty analysis, and not wanting to disappoint Mr. Stevenson, I reached for the hem of my dress and lifted it, pleased to note that my hands were not trembling, at least not obviously, though from my burning cheeks I knew I was red as a tomato.

Mr. Vanier gave a low whistle of male appreciation, showing none of the restraint I had become so used to with Mr. Stevenson. "Sensational," he breathed. He glanced at Mr. Stevenson. "May I see more?"

"Certainly," Mr. Stevenson replied calmly, his eyes fixed on me. "Remove your dress, Olivia."

Just like that. Take off your clothes in front of this virtual stranger.

Thank goodness I was wearing my bra. Nevertheless, my first instinct was to refuse outright, as Mr. Stevenson had promised there'd be nothing sexual.

No, he hadn't, the voice in my head that keeps track of legal minutiae replied. He said nothing *overtly* sexual *directly* involving Mr. Vanier. And after all, he was only asking me to stand there. I'd already shown the man my garters. This was just a matter of degree. In for a penny, in for a pound.

My eyes on the ground, I reached back to unhook my dress and then dragged the zipper slowly down my back. I stepped out of the dress and set it on a nearby chair. Though even my ears were blushing at that point, I stood my ground, chin lifted, hands at my sides. I had done Mr. Stevenson's bidding with grace and self-control.

Mr. Vanier actually sighed. "Sheer perfection," he breathed. And while I knew this was an overstatement, I felt ridiculously pleased. Three babies, but I still had my figure.

My self-satisfaction was short-lived, however, because then Mr. Stevenson said, "Now the brassiere."

I glanced at Mr. Vanier. He was staring directly at me with an expression that reminded me of a hungry dog waiting to be tossed a bone. His hand had dropped down to his lap, covering the obvious bulge there.

I swallowed hard as I gathered my courage. Was I really prepared to bare my breasts for this man, however appreciative he might be? I looked directly at Mr. Stevenson, my mouth opening in protest, but I was stopped by his expression. It wasn't forbidding or demanding. It was happy. He looked as a happy as a boy who'd won a prized baseball card. I understood then that this wasn't just about testing me. He was delighted to show his friend that I belonged to him, and he was proud to possess me in this unusual way.

Suddenly, I desperately wanted to earn the pride he felt for me—for what we shared. I wanted to please him above all things. My hands were trembling, but I somehow managed to fumble with my bra hooks. I let my bra slip down my arms. There I stood, wearing only panties, stockings and heels. The air was cool against my nipples. Impulse overcame obedience and I covered my chest.

"Drop your arms, slave."

Slave.

The word skipped right past my brain and settled in that warm, dark core of my essence. Feeling somehow calmer, I let my arms fall to my sides. I cast another glance at Mr. Vanier, who was leaning forward, his lips parted, a glazed look in his eyes.

Thank goodness, Mr. Stevenson stopped there with the forced striptease, because I honestly don't think I could have removed my underwear. Instead, he said, "Go to the corner, Olivia," his voice quiet but commanding. "Touch your forehead to the wall and assume the punishment position."

Slowly I walked to the corner, my heart racing a mile a minute. I stopped a few feet in front of the wall and bent over at the waist. My legs felt like they were made of rubber, no bones to speak of. I was finding it hard to balance in my heels.

Mr. Stevenson must have noticed, because he said, "You may step out of your shoes."

Thank goodness for small mercies.

I slipped them off and laced my fingers behind my head as Mr. Stevenson had taught me, my legs parted, my bottom thrust out. I felt incredibly vulnerable and exposed, far more so than when it was just us two, but also deeply excited, so much so that I had trouble catching my breath.

Behind me, Mr. Stevenson said, "My slave girl sometimes requires a good spanking. I reserve the ruler for punishments, but I like to use my hand for training. It reminds her of her place."

Oh. My. God.

I was glad I was facing away from the men, because my face was so hot you could have fried an egg on it.

"She's got a great ass, James," Mr. Vanier replied. "You are one lucky devil. Think I could give it a try?"

"Certainly," Mr. Stevenson replied, calm as you please. "I'll get her warmed up for you."

I very nearly dropped my arms and bolted out of there. This wasn't part of the deal. I wasn't supposed to have to do anything overtly sexual with Mr. Vanier. But then, one could argue that a spanking wasn't *overtly* sexual.

As I engaged in this internal debate, Mr. Stevenson came up behind me. He leaned close to my ear, and I could smell his warm, comforting scent. "Courage," he said softly. "You're doing beautifully. I have never been prouder in my life."

His words both thrilled and calmed me. I gave a small nod. I could do this. I would earn his pride.

He took a step back and I tensed in anticipation. The first smack was quite hard, the sound ringing in the room. I gasped but held my position, keenly aware Mr. Vanier was watching. He alternated cheeks, hard as you like, until I was panting, my bottom on fire, my sex too.

After about ten swats, he took a step back. "Would you care to continue? She can take quite a bit."

"Boy, would I," Mr. Vanier said enthusiastically. "I'd like her over my lap. Would that be all right, do you think?"

Mr. Stevenson leaned close to me and said softly, "Would you permit that, Olivia? It's beyond the parameters of our original agreement. I'll only allow it if you are comfortable with that."

I guess I was so surprised at being asked my permission that I replied, "Yes, that would be okay, Sir." Not to mention, my arms were growing tired, and my forehead kept slipping against the wall.

"Excellent. You may lower your arms and turn around."

He turned to Mr. Vanier. "Olivia has given her consent to that arrangement."

Mr. Vanier lifted his eyebrows. "Consent? I thought she was your slave."

"Within specific parameters, yes. It is a voluntary exchange of power, negotiated in advance. I'm sure you understand, given the nature of our, uh, external situations."

"Right, of course," Mr. Vanier agreed, trying to affect a sober expression, though I could see he was eager as a schoolboy to get his chance.

As Mr. Vanier moved from his chair to the couch, Mr. Stevenson led me over to him as if I were made of china and helped me drape myself over his friend's lap.

Mr. Vanier stroked me, his hand warm and damp over my panties. I believe he was even more nervous than I. He smacked me in a playful way at first, but soon was striking me harder, his breath coming in quick, excited spurts, his erection hard as a rock beneath me.

My flesh was already tender from Mr. Stevenson's spanking, and soon I was squirming on Mr. Vanier's lap, unable to stay still as he struck me harder and harder. I began to gasp, small, yelping sounds with each smack.

Then his hand strayed down between my legs, which had fallen apart during the spanking. I slammed them together, completely pulled out of the moment by his presumption.

"That's enough now, George," Mr. Stevenson said abruptly, obviously having witnessed what he'd done. "Olivia's had enough."

Mr. Vanier's hands fell away, and I stood, rather too quickly. The blood rushed from my head, and I swayed, black spots in front of my eyes for a few seconds.

Mr. Stevenson's strong arms came around me. "You were wonderful," he said softly. "Take your things and get dressed. Then come back to us, dear. We'll be waiting."

More later, because the bus, unlike Mr. Stevenson, won't wait.

~*~

Tess was sprawled across Ryan's bed, eyes closed, one hand partially covering her face, her dark hair spread over the pillow. The coverlet had fallen away to reveal one perfect breast, the nipple a pretty pink against soft, creamy skin. A breeze from the open window ruffled the curtains. Tess shifted but didn't wake.

Ryan liked watching her sleep, her face so peaceful in repose. His cock stirred at the memory of last night—of Tess, naked and bound in chains, completely at his mercy, her eyes closed, her lips parted and glistening, her body covered in a sheen of sweat, her nipples dark red and engorged. He could almost hear her sweet, sexy moans as the leather lashed against her flesh.

The raw, dominant power coursing through his blood as he'd flogged her still resonated through his being. She had given herself completely to the situation—to him—in a way that left no room for doubt. She was born for this, as was he.

He'd been cautious at first, afraid of hurting her, of moving too quickly from pleasure to erotic pain. Though he loved what they were exploring together, it was new for him, too. But she had led him, in her quiet and sexy way, giving clear cues that she wanted what he was offering. The sex afterward had been explosive—more powerful than anything he'd known in his life. The flogging had been extended foreplay, and the thrill and intensity of the experience had opened his eyes to what true lovemaking could be.

And it was just the beginning.

He slipped from the bed and washed up in the bathroom, moving quietly so as not to disturb her. When he came back out, she was still fast asleep. He stood a while longer, admiring the lovely, sleeping girl, until his need for coffee got the better of him. In the kitchen, as he measured the beans and ground them, he lost himself in pleasant daydreams.

Until Tess had entered his life, Ryan had sometimes wondered if there was anyone out there for him. In the past, his relationships seemed to take two steps forward, and then one step back. When there started to be more backward progress than forward, one or the other of them would eventually call it quits. While he'd loved these other women, something had always been missing. In his heart of hearts, or no, more accurately, in his soul of souls, he'd been waiting for "the one."

With Tess, there had been no false moves between them. The trust had been immediate and profound. For the first time, he understood on a gut level what a soul mate really meant. He was always learning something new and wonderful when he was with her, not only about her, but about himself. He loved her optimism and her zest for experience. Most of all, he loved her passion and her trust as they moved together deeper into BDSM.

Ryan was shaken out of his reverie by the sound of the garage door opening. What the hell? Peter wasn't due back until the next day. Ryan panicked for a moment, thinking of the chains still hanging from the ceiling in the exercise room, the flogger lying where it had been dropped.

The door from the garage opened, and Peter stepped into the kitchen. "Surprise," he said with a grin. "I'm back early." Peter, who stood at six-foot five, was long-limbed and narrow. He sometimes reminded Ryan of a praying mantis, especially when he unfolded himself from a chair or car that was too small for him.

"What're you doing here?" Ryan blurted. "You weren't due back until tomorrow."

"Hey, it's great to see you too, pal." Peter's grin fell away as he added, "The trip was a bust and I called it quits. The prospective clients had no business plan and no clear idea of what they were doing. Worse, I suspect some book cooking." Peter was a venture capital guy who found promising companies and helped them package themselves to get loans and capital. He was doing well now and had plans to move out soon and get a place of his own.

"Anyway"—he shrugged his overnight bag off his shoulder—"I'm hungry. What you got there?" He shook his head dismissively when Ryan held up a loaf of bread. "I need food, buddy. I'll make some pancakes. You up for that?"

Ryan, who was always up for Peter's cooking, said eagerly, "You bet."

Peter leaned into the refrigerator and pulled out milk and eggs. "Ah, and these strawberries should do nicely."

"Tess is here," Ryan said. "She should be up soon, so make enough for her."

Peter swung around to grin at him. "So you finally brought her home, huh? Must be serious. I can't wait to meet her. I'm glad to hear she eats pancakes. Does she have a sister?" Peter's girlfriend was on a constant diet, a source of frustration for Peter, who was a gourmet cook.

"I'll go see if she's up." Ryan made a quick detour to grab the flogger and spreader bar from the exercise room. Maybe Peter, who didn't go into that room much, wouldn't notice the chains, and if he did, so what. It was Ryan's house, after all. He could do as he liked.

Tess was in the shower, and he warned her Peter had come back early. "He's making strawberry pancakes, though, so I told him I wouldn't kill him."

"As long as there's real maple syrup, oh, and some bacon, I guess it's okay," Tess said with a laugh.

"I'll go make sure," Ryan said, his heart swelling with love.

Chapter 10

January 4, 1962

Holy cow. Is it really 1962 already? I swear, each year goes faster than the last. Mr. Stevenson gave me two weeks off for the kids' Christmas break. Of course, the family time was wonderful, but, though I must be a terrible mother for admitting this, a part of me was longing to get back to work, or, more accurately, back to Mr. Stevenson. I felt guilty about this, naturally, and really tried to focus on the family. But there you are.

I need to get to what I wanted to write about. I did something I never thought I'd do. Not because I find it disgusting, but because Frank would have been horrified at the thought of me doing it. I suspect he isn't horrified in general at the idea—I know about the Playboy magazines he keeps hidden in his workbench—but I think the concept of his *wife* doing it is more than he could handle.

Here's what happened.

I've been back at work since Tuesday, and the first two days we were so busy catching up with mail and dictation that there was very little time for any hanky-panky. We began to ease back into some of our sexier routines after that, including several painful but exciting bouts with the ruler on my bare bottom. But then this morning, Mr. Stevenson upped the ante. Boy, oh boy, did he!

"Today," he intoned in that formal way he has, "will be a new test of your submission. I am going to teach you the art of fellatio."

Fellatio.

It sounds like a character in an Italian opera. My first reaction was to refuse outright. There was no way I was going to get on my knees and put my mouth on that man's penis. And I said so, in no uncertain terms.

He lifted his eyebrows, a smile playing over his lips. He waited several beats and then said in a gentle tone, "Olivia, who do you belong to?"

I admit it—I love when he says that. There's something so sexy and intense about it. And the way he says it, so soft and low, like a caress.

"You, Sir," I whispered, unable to help myself.

He nodded slowly and then asked, "Do you understand, when you refuse something I want, that you are saying, through your actions, that you don't trust me? That whatever is going on between us is really just playacting to satisfy your sexual whims?"

I stared at him, at a loss for words.

He was right, of course. I love the game, as long as it's my rules we're playing by. I can pretend to be submissive all I want, but when he asks me to do something I don't want to do, or am afraid to do, I balk.

He didn't press me. Instead, he said, "I want you to take a day to think about it. I'm not going to force you. You will have to come to this of your own free will. Our exchange of power is a voluntary one. Here's what I want you to think about—do you want to keep things just as they are between us, or are you ready to move to a higher plane of submission, one where you truly surrender, truly give of yourself?"

I didn't reply, not sure what to say, though I could already feel some of my outraged resolve slipping away.

"We'll revisit the subject in the morning, Olivia. When you're ready, you will ask me if you may suck my cock."

Suck his cock! It sounds so obscene. I'm not even sure it's legal.

But that was the end of it. He spent most of the day in his office, the door closed, while I clacked away on my typewriter, did some filing and handled phone calls. At first, I was just plain annoyed. Sometimes I think he's full of boloney. He puts these ideas in my head and couches them in lofty sentiment, just to get what he wants. But then, I get to thinking...

January 5, 1962

He has this way of working on me, like he's planting these seeds in me that burst into flower when I'm not watching. I couldn't stop thinking about this whole idea of what he wants me to do. A part of me is actually quite curious, from a physiological standpoint. What would it be like? Could I even do it?

And then there's the psychological aspect. From what I know of this, the man kind of loses control. He's in seventh heaven, completely under the spell of the woman who is pleasuring him. Talk about power! For once, I'd be the one in control. At least, as in control as one can be when on her knees.

I was considering it. I really was.

But, when he asked me if I was ready to submit to his wish, the words just popped out like popcorn. "No, Sir. I am not."

January 8, 1962

When he came into the office this morning, after I'd spent the entire weekend silently obsessing about what I would or wouldn't do, I blurted out, "I'm ready, Sir. I want to do it."

In classic Mr. Stevenson style, he cocked his head slightly, as if confused, though I was damn sure he knew just exactly what I was saying. "I'm sorry, what? What is it you want to do?"

"You know," I hedged. Was he really going to make me say it?

"I may know," he replied calmly as he hung up his hat, "but I want you to tell me. What is it you want to do?"

"What we talked about last week. About your, uh, your cock," I mumbled.

"Speak clearly, Olivia," he said, not even trying to hide his smile. "Are you asking me for permission to suck my cock?"

Heat seared across my face, while at the same time, I can't deny it, I got that achy feeling I get in my sex when he asserts control. He wouldn't let up until I said the words he wanted to hear. Somehow, I forced myself to say, "I want to suck your cock, Sir."

"That's good to hear, Olivia. I'm pleased. I'll call you in when I'm ready for you."

Typical.

Anticipation is key, he likes to say. As I sat at my desk, trying to work, I could barely sit still. I stuck a hand in my panties right there at my desk. I rubbed a little and it felt good. I was thinking of heading into the bathroom to do the job properly, when he called out, "Olivia."

Excited and nervous as a cat, I came into his office. Mr. Stevenson was standing in front of the couch. His jacket was off, but he was otherwise fully clothed. He sat down and said, "Come here and kneel before me, slave."

My heart already going a mile a minute, I obeyed, letting that lovely net of submissive release settle over me.

He took a handkerchief from his pocket and set it beside him. "Open my belt and my pants."

I managed to unbuckle his belt and unzip his pants without too much fumbling.

He pulled his shirt and undershirt out of the way and reached into the fly of his boxers. When he pulled out his cock, I nearly bolted from the room, but I gathered my courage and stayed put. I looked up at him, expecting some kind of direction, but he just said, "Go ahead."

Taking a deep breath, I squeezed my eyes shut and stuck my tongue out in the general direction of his penis.

Mr. Stevenson chuckled. "For God's sake, Olivia. It's not going to bite you." He took my head gently in his hands as he peered down at me. "I want you to make love to my cock, Olivia. To worship it as a sign of your devotion. You can do it. Do it for me. Relax and open your throat, and take pleasure in the knowledge that you're pleasing me."

His voice, his words—they struck a perfect, resonant chord in me, and my tensed muscles relaxed, my pulse slowing.

At first, I just kind of licked around the head and then drew my tongue along the shaft. He smelled good—like Ivory soap and his own musky essence. There was a fat vein on the underside that throbbed against my tongue.

He sighed with obvious pleasure and leaned back, his eyes closing.

I was instantly pleased with myself. I had a glimpse of what it must be like to dominate another—to take control and reduce someone to pure lust and need, as he so often does with me.

I continued a while longer, licking along the smooth, satiny skin, until he placed his hands on my shoulders and looked down at me. "You're doing well, Olivia. Now, I want you to take it into your mouth. You may cradle my balls and the base of the shaft with your hands, gently. Take your time. Start with the head and move slowly down. Open your throat and stay relaxed. I understand this is new and difficult for you, and I'm honored with this gift of your submission."

Suddenly, all I wanted was to please him.

I kept gagging when I tried to take it in too far. Still, whatever I was doing must have been okay, because it wasn't long before he began to breathe heavily, and I could actually feel his balls tightening in my hand. I started to panic when I could tell he was about to climax. The thought of him ejaculating into my mouth was—is—so disgusting that I was afraid I'd end up spitting it out and making a scene.

He must have sensed my sudden tension in the rigidity of my body, because he said, "Don't worry, darling, I won't come in your mouth. Not this time." Then he took my head in his hands and began to move his cock in and out of my mouth.

It was weird, because I'm used to being the one who loses control, but now it was he, my Master, who was moaning and panting. All at once, he pulled back and grabbed his handkerchief, his face twisted in orgasmic pleasure. With a cry, he spurted his seed into the handkerchief and then fell back against the cushions, still breathing heavily. He looked like such a sweet mess, disheveled and exposed.

Along with a rising sense of feminine triumph, I felt an extraordinary tenderness toward Mr. Stevenson.

Toward James.

He looked down at me, something raw and vulnerable in his face.

Then he whispered, "I love you."

~*~

It was Sunday morning, and they'd slept in, a rare event for either of them. After another delicious breakfast prepared by Peter, they'd returned to the bedroom for some lovemaking and journal reading.

"Hey, don't stop," Ryan said as Tess closed the last of the notebooks. "I need to know what happens next."

Tess flipped through the last few pages again, just in case she'd missed something, but they were blank. "That's it." A sense of loss moved through her at the thought that these were the last of Olivia's secret diaries. "That's all she wrote."

Ryan scrunched his face. "That can't be it. She called him James. He said he loved her. I'm starting to understand why there are so many women who love romances. I'm totally into this."

Tess laughed, but then shook her head as she stroked the cover of the pale blue notebook, sad to think the window into Olivia's past was closing for them. Tess was going to miss the ritual of sharing Olivia's story with Ryan.

"These are all I found in that strongbox," she said, recalling the day of her discovery. "But you have to be right. That can't be all there was between them. After all, he called the house right after she died."

"Do you still have access to your grandmother's house?"

Tess nodded. "Yeah. I still have a key. It's about to be put up for sale, though. My mom has ordered a dumpster and they're going to toss everything left that can't be sold when the place goes on the market."

He swung his legs over the edge of the bed with determination. "Then we better get over there pronto and tear that attic apart, just in case you missed something the first time around. If there are more of these precious gems hidden away, we need to find them before they're inadvertently thrown out."

"Or found by someone else, like my mom," Tess said, catching Ryan's sense of urgency. "Let's go."

After over two hours of scouring every nook and cranny, not only of the attic, but the basement and every room in the house, they were forced to admit defeat. "If they existed," Ryan said, "they don't anymore. We'll never get the full story of the Master and the secretary."

"Well, we know one thing for sure—my grandparents never split up, so they kept the affair secret. You know," she added, staring contemplatively out the kitchen window, "I think that last entry was a game changer. The relationship between them was shifting to something a lot more intimate. It's one thing to write a journal about some kinky games played at the office, but I imagine it would be quite another to document a real love affair."

Ryan nodded thoughtfully. "I bet you're right." He took Tess into his arms and kissed her nose. Then he pulled back, capturing her in his green-eyed gaze. "We're at a similar crossroad as James and Olivia, you and I. We're both ready to move to something more intense—more profound."

"Yes," Tess replied softly. She was at once terrified and thrilled to her bones at the thought of giving herself so completely to another. "I want that, too, but I have to confess, sometimes I'm scared. At the same time, I feel more alive than I ever have in my life. I feel, so—this may sound weird—but so brave and empowered. It's like we're exploring a whole new world together. Though, obviously, it's been explored before." She sighed, thinking again of Olivia and her Mr. Stevenson.

"She was an amazing woman, your nana," Ryan said gently, as if reading Tess's mind. "And you're amazing, too. And yes, I get it that you're scared sometimes. This is new, scary stuff, but that doesn't make it bad. It takes courage to submit. I'm asking you to give up control, and that requires a lot of trust. I promise to always be worthy of that trust, Tess," he said softly, again taking her into his arms. "We're becoming, together, what we were always meant to be." He dipped his head and kissed her.

The ringing landline made them, reluctantly, pull away from one another. "Huh," Tess said, moving toward the wall-mounted, old-fashioned phone. "I wonder who that could be." She picked up the receiver. "Hello?"

There was a pause, during which Tess almost hung up, and then a deep, resonant voice said, "Tess? Is this Tess Shepard?"

Tess's heart began to pound. Even before her conscious mind processed who was on the phone, she knew. "Yes," she managed to stammer, "This is she."

"This is James Stevenson. I don't know if you remember, but we spoke, very briefly, a few weeks back when you…when you gave me the terrible news."

"Yes, of course I remember," she replied, managing to keep her voice steady and even. "I'm so sorry you had to find out that way." She recalled the shock and heartbreak in his voice that, at the time, she hadn't fully understood. "But how did you know my name? Or that I'd be here?"

Ryan had moved to stand by her, his eyebrows raised in question.

"It's Mr. Stevenson," she mouthed silently, letting her incredulity show in her face.

"No way," Ryan breathed softly. "What the hell?"

She shrugged to indicate she had no idea, and then focused on the man's words.

"I hope you don't mind my calling you. I had your mother's phone number, and she told me I might find you at Olivia's place. I believe I'd mentioned during our first conversation that Olivia and I were old friends."

And a *whole* lot more, Tess immediately thought, but of course didn't voice.

"Olivia spoke of you fondly and often, more than anyone else in her family."

Grateful tears filled Tess's eyes, and she wiped them away. Ryan put his arm around her, and she leaned into him.

"I called because... well, frankly because I'm seeking a way of closure, having missed her funeral service. I'm having trouble processing the fact that your grandmother is no longer in the world." He cleared his throat. "Forgive me, I'm still somewhat emotional over the loss."

"Not at all," she replied, still not sure what he was seeking.

"I hope you won't find this request too odd, but I was wondering if we could meet, perhaps for dinner?"

It was as if the universe, having denied Tess any more of Olivia's journals, was giving her the next best thing—a chance to meet the real Mr. Stevenson in the flesh. How could she possibly refuse?

"I'd be delighted to meet you," she replied sincerely. "I'd like to bring my boyfriend, Ryan Hunter, if that's all right."

"That's perfectly fine," Mr. Stevenson agreed readily. "Are the two of you available for dinner tomorrow evening?"

Tess put her hand over the receiver and murmured to Ryan, "Dinner, tomorrow night with Mr. Stevenson?"

"Absolutely," Ryan said emphatically. "Holy shit."

"Yes," Tess said, grinning into the phone. "That would work. Did you have a place in mind?"

"Do you know *Le Coq*, downtown?"

"I do, but I'm not sure we could get reservations on such short notice," Tess replied. *Le Coq* was a very high-end restaurant that was famous for three-month waiting lists for reservations, not to mention ridiculously high prices.

"Not to worry," Mr. Stevenson said smoothly. "I am good friends with the chef. This will be my treat, and my pleasure. Shall we say seven o'clock?"

"Sounds like a plan," Tess agreed.

"Thank you again. I look forward to meeting you and Ryan."

As they were getting dressed the next evening, Ryan said, "Do you trust me with your submission, Tess?"

She drew in a sharp breath, the thrill of his words reverberating inside her. "Yes, Sir," she said softly.

"Tonight, if it feels right, I may ask you for a display of that submission in front of Mr. Stevenson."

"What?" she blurted, stopping midway through putting on her earrings. "What do you mean?"

"Well, we both know that Mr. Stevenson is hardwired like we are. He's a Dom, and he demonstrated pretty clearly in those journals that he's very comfortable in the role."

"But he's—he's so old. He must be over ninety."

"So?" Ryan countered. "You know the old saying—a tiger doesn't change his stripes. These kinds of feelings and desires we share—they don't just go away, I'm sure of it."

"Okay," Tess said slowly. "So what would, um, a display of submission mean exactly?"

Ryan smiled, his eyes sparking in a way that sent a shiver through Tess's body. "I'm not sure, *exactly*. That's why I'm asking for your trust. If it feels right, I'd like to show him what we share—that you belong to me, much as Olivia once belonged to him." He came over to her and took her into his arms, adding, "Though we're so much luckier, because we don't have to hide our love."

He ran his finger down her cheek and along her jawline. Then he placed his hand lightly around her throat as he peered into her soul. The primal touch sent another shudder coursing through Tess's loins. As he tightened his grip, she couldn't help herself—she moaned aloud.

"Is that a yes?" Ryan teased, a small, sexy smile playing over his lips.

"Yes," Tess breathed, electrified with fear and desire in equal measure. "Yes, Sir."

The maître d' looked down his nose as Ryan and Tess approached the host station. "Ryan Hunter and Tess Shepard," Ryan said smoothly. "We're meeting Mr. James Stevenson."

The man's expression instantly softened into a deferential smile. "Ah, Mr. Stevenson. He has already been seated." He nodded toward the young woman standing beside him. "Angela will show you to his table."

The large room was elegantly appointed, with linen tablecloths and subtle lighting, every table occupied. Toward the back in a discreet corner, an imposing older gentleman sat alone at a table set for three. He still had a full head of silver hair brushed back from a high forehead. When he looked up, his eyes, though faded, were still blue, and his face creased into a smile as they approached.

He got slowly to his feet and reached out to take Tess's hand. "You must be Tess," he said in that deep, resonant voice Tess had so often imagined when they'd read Olivia's journals. "What a pleasure to meet you at last. I feel as if I already know you."

"It's nice to meet you," Tess replied, slightly awestruck at seeing Mr. Stevenson in the flesh.

Dropping her hand, he turned to Ryan. As they shook, Ryan said, "I'm Ryan Hunter. A pleasure to make your acquaintance, Mr. Stevenson."

"Likewise. And please, call me James."

A waiter appeared instantly before them. Ryan and Tess each ordered a glass of wine, while Mr. Stevenson requested a martini with two olives. They spent a few minutes exchanging pleasantries and backgrounds, with Mr. Stevenson noting he'd retired from his law practice some twenty years before, and now lived a quiet life, enjoying his solitude and taking pleasure in his grandchildren when they visited. He was very interested in Ryan's and Tess's law careers and asked lots of questions about what it was like to practice in today's environment.

"Olivia had a very sharp legal mind, you know. She would have been an excellent attorney in her own right," he remarked.

"Nana was sharp as a tack," Tess agreed. *But tell us about your affair. How long did it last? How far did it go?* She was dying to ask, but didn't dare.

The food was delicious, and Mr. Stevenson couldn't get enough of Tess's childhood stories about Olivia. He kept refilling Tess's wine glass, and she drank more than she was used to. She had a definite buzz going by the time the main course was cleared away.

As they were waiting for coffee and dessert, it must have been the liquor that loosened her tongue, because the words slipped out before she could censor them. "We found the journals, you know. The secret diaries."

Both men stared at her, Ryan with an amused smile, Mr. Stevenson with confusion. Then, all at once, he seemed to understand, and his face grew pale. Tess desperately wished she could stuff the words back into her mouth, but it was too late. Ryan, no doubt sensing her distress, put his hand over hers and gave it a little squeeze.

Mr. Stevenson seemed to compose himself, and after a moment, he said quietly, "She still had them, after all these years?"

There was no point in trying to backtrack at this point. "Yes. I found them after she died," Tess said. "They were locked in a strongbox in the attic. I'm sure no one but she had ever seen them," she hastened to add.

"Until you, I suppose you mean? You read her secret, private journals?" Mr. Stevenson's tone was more bewildered than anything.

Shame rushed through Tess's veins. There was no doubt—Ryan and she had trespassed into someone else's very private life. It was like peeking in on lovers who didn't know you were there. She turned helplessly to Ryan, not sure how to respond.

Ryan gave her a reassuring smile and addressed Mr. Stevenson. "Let's put things in perspective. If you had discovered old tracts of writing buried in your relative's attic, wouldn't you have done the same? Tess loved her grandmother with all her heart. Imagine being offered the chance after someone you love has just died to somehow connect with them again, to perhaps know them a little better, for a little longer. In Tess's position, would you have denied yourself that chance?"

Mr. Stevenson, who had been gripping his glass tightly, released it and sat back, his color returning. He smiled. "You've made your point. And yes, given the situation you have described, I doubt I could have resisted the temptation." He looked steadily at Ryan. "I assume you read them, as well."

"Yes," Ryan admitted, gazing back. "I apologize for imposing on your privacy in that way. Tess was seeking a connection with Olivia, and she wanted to share that with me. The truly astonishing thing is how strongly Tess and I connected with you both—with the exploration of Dominance and submission." He reached for Tess's hand under the table. "Tess and I are on the same path, if that puts your mind more at rest. Olivia's journals gave us permission, in a way, to deepen our own exploration into D/s."

Mr. Stevenson raised his eyebrows. "Is that so?" he said slowly, looking from Ryan to Tess, gazing at her in a way that made her want to look away, though somehow, she was unable to.

He broke the spell by reaching for his water glass. He took a sip and set his glass down carefully. "I never read them, you know. She stopped writing in them after the first year or so. After"—he paused, a wistful expression coming onto his face—"things changed between us."

Tell us more, Tess silently begged, but managed to hold her tongue.

Mr. Stevenson smiled, though the sadness lingered in his eyes. "When I saw her scribbling away, sometimes I would tease her that she was taking notes for a great novel she would someday publish. She would laugh and tell me to mind my own business. For a submissive, she could be pretty bossy."

"She could be pretty bossy for a grandmother, too," Tess said with a laugh, missing Olivia something fierce.

"I'd like to hear more about what you said about your own exploration in D/s," Mr. Stevenson said. "That is, if you'd care to share."

Ryan again took Tess's hand underneath the table, giving it a slight squeeze, as if asking permission from her. She squeezed back, granting it, though butterflies had begun to dance in her stomach. Was this when the "demonstration" Ryan had promised would take place?

"We're both pretty new to the scene," Ryan said, "at least in terms of acting on our desires and impulses. I've always had dominant feelings, but I hadn't really found the right partner to explore it with until I met Tess." He gave her hand another comforting squeeze and glanced at her.

Taking her cue, she added, "I had never really articulated my submissive feelings, even to myself, until I started reading Olivia's journals. Ryan has been amazing, always there to take me to the next level when I'm ready. It just feels...right, if you know what I mean."

"I do know what you mean," Mr. Stevenson replied. "I envy your generation. You're so much freer, not only to explore, but to acknowledge these feelings in yourself, without the accompanying shame, confusion and guilt most people of my generation experienced." He fixed them each with those fierce blue eyes, looking from Ryan to Tess, and then back to Ryan. "Once Olivia became more comfortable in her role as my submissive, we found our relationship deepened when we shared that submission with others. I'm curious—have you found that to be the case in your relationship?"

"It's funny you should ask that," Ryan said as Tess's heart lurched into her throat. "We were discussing that concept this evening while we were getting ready. I mentioned to Tess I might ask her to demonstrate her submission in some way to a witness—to you."

Mr. Stevenson raised his eyebrows, again fixing Tess with his fiery gaze. "Indeed. I would love a demonstration." The timbre of his voice had changed, and she could feel the quiet power and authority in his tone.

Ryan's lips lifted in a slow, sexy smile. "I thought perhaps you might have something in mind, James."

Tess felt dizzy, and it was only partially from the wine. Was this really happening? Could she handle it? Did she want to?

Yes, a sure, steady voice whispered from deep in her core. *I want it. I need it.*

Mr. Stevenson looked thoughtful. "We are in a public place, so of course you'll need to be discreet. I suggest something simple—a small testament of her desire to please you—something that will test her submission in a concrete way."

"An excellent suggestion." Ryan turned to Tess. "Take off your panties and hand them to Mr. Stevenson."

"Right here? Right now?" Tess blurted, reflexively glancing to the left and right of their table.

Ryan lifted his eyebrows. "Do you have a problem obeying me, Tess?"

Tess bit her lip, her breath catching in her throat.

Ryan gently cupped her cheek as he stared into her eyes in that way he had that left her weak in the knees. Her body and soul yielded to him, opening and softening like a flower in bloom. "No, Sir," she whispered.

She stared down at the table as she reached beneath the tablecloth. With another anxious glance around her, Tess lifted her bottom, praying the waiter wouldn't choose that moment to reappear at their table. As she removed her panties, hot, sweet humiliation melted her from the inside out.

Mission accomplished, she extended her arm underneath the table toward Mr. Stevenson, her panties bunched in her fist.

"No," Ryan interjected. "Not under the table. I want to see you give your panties to this gentleman."

Face flaming, Tess handed the wadded-up bit of silk to Mr. Stevenson in plain sight of anyone who might have been looking.

He accepted it with a solemn nod. "Thank you, Tess. You are as courageous as your grandmother was." He slipped the panties into the inner pocket of his suit jacket and then smiled broadly at Ryan.

Ryan squeezed Tess's thigh under the table as he leaned over to kiss her cheek, and happiness flooded through her being.

The waiter appeared with their coffee and dessert. Once he had gone, Mr. Stevenson regarded Tess with a thoughtful expression, though when he spoke, it was to Ryan. "Is Tess also a sexual masochist?"

"She is," Ryan said without even looking at her. "Though we're still exploring her limits in that regard."

Tess flushed anew at the way they were discussing her as if she were a toy or...or a slave... She felt at once hot and cold, heated by the sexual fire in her core, while at the same time frightened by the icy sensation of being so objectified by these two men.

"How wonderful for you both," Mr. Stevenson said.

The waiter appeared, placing a bill folder next to Mr. Stevenson's plate, and the strange, sensual netting that had dropped over Tess's senses melted away as the mood shifted.

Mr. Stevenson reached into his jacket and took out a slim leather wallet. He placed an American Express Black Card on the folder without even glancing at the bill. As the waiter whisked it away, he took a business card from his wallet and handed it to Ryan. "I do hope we can meet again. This dinner has been most"—he patted his jacket pocket where Tess's panties now resided—"delightful."

Chapter 11

As they drove home from the restaurant, Ryan ran his hand along Tess's smooth thigh, inching her dress up as he did so. He loved knowing she was naked underneath her skirt. "You were incredible tonight." He glanced from the road to Tess. "I'm so proud of you, and I'm honored by the grace with which you submitted to me in front of a witness."

"Thank you," she said softly, but instead of meeting his eye, she looked away.

"What? What is it, sweetheart?"

"Nothing. Nothing, really," she mumbled.

"Obviously it's something," he replied. "Please, Tess. Talk to me. Did I read your cues wrong? Did I force you into something you weren't comfortable with? If I did, you need to tell me."

She flashed him a grateful look. "No, it was fine." She gave a small laugh. "More than fine—it was really exciting. But it was also"—she paused, apparently gathering her thoughts—"weird."

"Weird, how?"

"Your conversation—the two of you. The way you talked about me as if I weren't even there. Or no, as if I were an object. A toy. A...slave."

"And you didn't like that?"

"It's not that I didn't like it," she replied thoughtfully. "That's what was weird. It was more than *like*. On a deep, submissive level, I *adored* it. I got this strange, sexy feeling, almost like I wasn't even me, or I was a different me. Shit." She gave an exasperated laugh. "I don't know how to describe it. It's like I entered this different place—a different headspace, if that make any sense."

"A submissive headspace, maybe?" Ryan offered.

"Yes. But in that space, I sort of got lost. I mean, I felt like I was almost an extension of you—your sex slave, doing your bidding. I was in a kind of altered state. It was...I guess it was scary, giving myself over like that. I'm-I'm not used to it."

"Surrender is definitely scary," Ryan agreed. "I think it takes enormous courage to submit—way more than to dominate," he said sincerely. "I admire you tremendously, Tess. You weren't only graceful and sexy as hell in your submission tonight, you were courageous."

"Thank you," she said, flashing him a beautiful smile. "But here's the thing. I keep thinking about Charlotte, in that book you gave me. She was objectified to the point she no longer existed outside of the confines of being Sir Jonathan's sex slave. She lost her identity, except in the context of serving and pleasing him. I don't think I could do that, Ryan. I don't want to do that."

"And I wouldn't want you to do that," Ryan said, reaching to find her hand. "I know exactly what you're saying about Charlotte, but remember, that was stylized fiction, written a long time ago when D/s was still regarded as a perversion. Sir Jonathan and Charlotte were archetypes, not real people. What we're doing is real life. And don't forget, we have something they never had. We have love, Tess. And that will make all the difference."

Tess lifted his hand to her lips, turning it over to kiss his palm. "Thank you, Ryan. You're right, love is the key."

When they got back to her apartment, Ryan undressed her, directing her to stand still as he slowly removed each article of clothing. When she was naked, he had her lie down on her back on the bed.

"Spread your arms and legs wide. I'm going to tie you down."

"Yes, Sir," Tess breathed, her nipples instantly hardening into gumdrops he couldn't help but kiss. She moaned sweetly as he licked and suckled at her breasts, her arms and legs spread obediently along the mattress.

Crouching beside the bed, he pulled out the storage container they now kept under her bed, which they were slowly filling with BDSM toys and implements. He removed several coils of rope, along with a small red riding crop. He set the crop on the carpet and pushed the container back under the bed. Leaning up, he bound her wrists first in easily removable knots, tying off the rope on either side of the bedframe.

He got to his feet, admiring how beautiful and vulnerable she looked. Quickly, he stripped off his clothing and tossed it aside. Before tying her ankles, he slipped a pillow beneath her ass and directed her to spread her legs so he would have good access to her beautiful, flower-bud pussy, which she'd shaved smooth for him. Once her ankles were secured to either side of the bedframe, he sat beside her and pushed her thick, dark hair from her face.

"I love you, Tess," he murmured, and then he kissed her.

"I love you, Sir," she replied breathlessly when he released her.

Kneeling again beside the bed, he picked up the riding crop and drew the fold of leather down her abdomen, letting it rest against her smooth mons.

Tess drew in a small breath, a sexy shudder moving through her frame.

"I'm going to whip your pretty little cunt," he said softly.

"Ryan," she gasped, her rich brown eyes widening with alarm. "You're not serious."

"Of course I am." He tapped very lightly against the pooching lips of her sex, pulling another sensual shudder from her. "But only with your permission, sub girl." He rubbed the head of the crop against her already swelling clit, stroking it with the soft leather.

She sighed. "That feels so good," she moaned, arching her hips wantonly to increase the friction.

Ryan chuckled, his cock hard as a rock in anticipation. "You're ready for more erotic pain, Tess, and I'm ready to give it to you." He lifted the crop and let it fall lightly between her legs, not enough to sting, but enough to get her attention.

She gasped softly and bit her lip, visibly swallowing, but she didn't protest.

"If things get too intense," he continued, "you always have your safeword, though I don't think you'll need it. Remember, I pay attention to your body and your cues. I'll only give you what you can handle." He let another stroke land, this one with slightly more force, thrilling to the sound of leather slapping moist flesh.

Again she gasped, but her nipples were hard points and a flush of desire was moving over her chest and cheeks.

"So, tell me, sub girl. Do I have your permission to crop your sweet, hot cunt?"

"Yes, Sir," she moaned. "Yes, please, Sir."

He began lightly, just a gentle tapping of leather against her spread pussy. Her hooded clit swelled as the leather stroked it, but when he let the first real sting land, Tess cried out and tried, unsuccessfully, to close her legs. She held the rope above her wrists in a white-knuckled grip, her breath a ragged pant.

"Relax your hands," Ryan directed. "Take deep, slow breaths. Stop fighting the crop. Settle into the erotic pain and let it envelop you."

He waited until she released her death-grip on the rope and managed to draw in several slow, deep breaths. Then he struck her again.

She yelped, again gripping the ropes for dear life.

He set down the crop and placed his hands over hers. "Relax, Tess," he said softly. "You're doing great." He stroked her swollen labia, drawing moisture from her entrance up over her hard clit. He knew just how to touch her, and he recognized the telltale signs of an impending climax, but she wasn't going to come. Not yet. Pulling his hand away, he said, "Shall I continue the cropping? Can you take more? Are you willing to suffer for me? Do you want to?"

She stared up at him with shining eyes. "Yes, Sir," she whispered. "I want to. Please."

He leaned over and kissed her mouth and then her eyelids.

She kept her eyes closed as he picked up the crop and let it fall lightly against her sex. She drew in a deep breath and let it out slowly.

"Good girl," he murmured. He settled into a steady, stinging rhythm, thrilled when Tess's cries began to edge from pain into breathless pleasure. "Oh god," she moaned. "It hurts, but it's so good. It's too much. I can't take it. Oh, oh, oh… I'm going to come!"

"Ask me," Ryan instructed, his cock aching as he continued to stroke her clit with the stinging leather.

"Please, Sir," she cried, panting. "May I come?"

"Yes."

He continued to strike her as she trembled and bucked, though with much lighter strokes, more of a caress than a whipping. Only when she sagged limply against the mattress, her eyes closed, her body covered in a light sheen of perspiration, did he throw the crop aside and drape himself hungrily over her.

Unable to restrain himself another second, he plunged into her wet, perfect heat. As her cunt spasmed around his cock, he groaned. He wanted to make it last, but he was too turned on by how passionately, how sexily, how submissively, she'd reacted to the pussy whipping, and, in less than a minute, he shuddered in his own release, calling out Tess's name as he let himself go.

~*~

Monday afternoon, Ryan stuck his head inside Tess's office. "Got a minute?"

Tess looked up with a smile. "Of course."

Ryan took a seat in front of her desk. "I spoke to Mr. Stevenson today."

Tess's heart did a sudden flip-flop. "You did?"

"Yep. And guess what? He and Olivia did continue their affair. Even after she retired, they still arranged to meet from time to time, all the way up until she died."

"Wow," Tess said. "That's over fifty years! I wonder why they didn't get together after Pop died? Mr. Stevenson was a widower by then," she mused aloud. "They could have had at least a year together—I mean really together, without having to hide it."

"I actually asked him that very question, but he was kind of vague in his response. I gathered from what he did say that they were both used to the arrangement as it was, and neither wanted to mess it up. Maybe they thought they'd ruin whatever special thing they had if they changed the formula. And maybe they would have, who knows?"

Tess was quiet as she thought about that. It wouldn't have been enough for her, but then, she hadn't walked in her grandmother's shoes.

"There's more," Ryan said, making her look up at him.

"What? Tell me."

Ryan leaned forward, clearly excited. "I wanted to see what you thought before I committed to anything. You might not be up for it, and if that's the case, it's totally cool. Even though you're my sub girl, you still have the power to say no if something makes you uncomfortable."

"I appreciate that," Tess replied, seething with curiosity. "Now tell me before I explode."

"James wanted to know more about what you and I have together. He wondered if you were at the point in your training—his word—that you would be ready for a further display of your submission to an outside observer."

"Ha," Tess interjected. "He got my panties, and now he wants more. He's just a dirty old man."

Ryan laughed. "And you're saying that's a bad thing?" He sobered, adding, "Seriously, though. It's not like that."

"I know," Tess said, still grinning. "I was teasing."

Ryan nodded. "But there is more to the story. Apparently George Vanier wasn't the only one Olivia was exposed to. Over the years, James regularly had men come into the office, and Olivia was required not only to display herself for these gentlemen, but eventually she was expected to service them—again his words."

"Whoa," Tess whispered, at once intrigued and horrified. But really, was the horror only because it had been her grandmother? Was moving from showing to doing just a natural progression in Mr. Stevenson and Olivia's D/s exploration? Was Olivia's giving herself to someone else at Mr. Stevenson's command the ultimate submission?

"So? What do you think? Would that be something you'd be interested in? I don't mean that you'd actually have sex with the guy," he added quickly. "But it would be intense if we allowed him to witness a scene between us."

"A scene?" Tess asked, at once deeply intrigued and nervous. "Like what?"

Ryan shrugged with feigned casualness, though his eyes were hooded and glittering in a way she had come to recognize meant he was very turned on. "I'll handle the specifics." His look became playful. "Don't worry—there'll be nothing overtly sexual." He grinned, obviously referring to Olivia's journal entry regarding Mr. Vanier.

Tess laughed. "As long as we have that straight," she quipped back.

Ryan sobered quickly, pinning her with a stare. "Just so we're clear, I'm not willing to share you sexually, even if Mr. Stevenson were up for it."

Tess grinned at the unintended pun, but let it pass.

"I'd like you to wear something sexy, but not *too* revealing," he continued. "I'm thinking that new waist cincher and thong panties."

"That's pretty darn revealing," Tess interjected, though she did absolutely love the black satin cincher he'd brought home for her, which gave her an hourglass figure and gorgeous cleavage.

"I *could* make you go naked," Ryan retorted with a grin. "After all, you belong to me."

His words unlocked something in her, despite his teasing tone. "Yes," she managed, her voice suddenly husky. "I do." And then, taking the leap into what promised to be a wild new adventure, she added, "And yes, I'll do it."

~*~

"He's in room 302. He said to go on up."

They approached the elevator together in the elegant, if now somewhat faded, downtown hotel where Mr. Stevenson and Olivia had met dozens of times over the many years of their liaison. Tess was biting her lower lip nervously, and Ryan could feel the tension in her body when he put his arm around her shoulders.

"Relax, sweetheart. Remember, in a D/s relationship, the sub is the one with the ultimate control. You are giving us the gift of your submission. If you're not comfortable at any time, no matter what, you tell me, okay? As much as we both like James and are excited at the prospect of a witness, we're under no obligation to him."

"I know," Tess agreed. "But at the same time, I wouldn't want to let him down. He's gone to a lot of trouble, getting the room and that portable suspension rig." She drew in a shuddery breath as she hugged herself, and Ryan knew she was thinking about the caning to come.

James and Ryan had spoken on the phone several times since their dinner meeting, and James had suggested that a cane was the next natural step in their exploration of erotic pain. When Ryan had broached the idea with Tess, she'd drawn in a sharp breath, her eyes widening, color rising in her cheeks. If she had refused, he wouldn't have pressed her. They had time—plenty of time.

But to his pleased surprise, she'd said, "I've been watching some videos online about caning. Some of them are brutal, but there's this one site called Sensual Pain that showed a couple, obviously amateurs, not actors, and they were both into it in a sexy, loving way that"—her blushed had deepened—"really got me going."

"Yeah?" Ryan had replied with a grin, intrigued. "And where was I when you were watching porn?"

"It wasn't porn," Tess had retorted with an embarrassed laugh. "It was education. I watched it when you were on that case that took you out of town for a night last week. I was bored."

The elevator doors glided open and they stepped into the empty car. As they ascended, Ryan placed his hands on Tess's shoulders and looked into her eyes. "Remember, you ultimately call the shots here."

She reached for him, circling her arms around his neck and pulling him down for a kiss. "Thank you, Sir," she said, before touching her lips to his. "I promise to make you proud."

~*~

Despite her intention to be brave and graceful, Tess's heart began to pound as Ryan knocked on the door of room 302. As if he'd been waiting on the other side, the door opened immediately, and there stood Mr. Stevenson, tall and still handsome despite his years, his blue eyes twinkling.

"Welcome," he said, taking a step back and ushering them inside. They briefly exchanged greetings and pleasantries, Tess on autopilot as she struggled to present a calm façade.

The aluminum suspension rig was already set up in the large room. It was a simple but effective-looking device, with three aluminum poles joined together at the top to form a kind of teepee. A metal bar hung from the apex by chains, Velcro cuffs secured at either end. A long, lethal-looking cane sat on the nearby desk beside an ice bucket that contained a bottle of champagne. Next to the bucket, there was a tray with three bottles of water and two champagne flutes.

Tess was in something of a daze, dizzy with nervous anticipation of what she'd agreed to, as the men discussed the parameters of the scene. She would be allowed to keep on the cincher and thong, though Mr. Stevenson suggested she remove her heels and stand in her bare feet for comfort and stability. Ryan would practice first with a pillow, before they moved to Tess's ass.

Yikes!

Tess had mixed feelings about being left out of the conversation. Her natural inclination as a woman who'd had to do everything twice as well as any male attorney to get noticed was to put in her two cents, but in her role as a submissive, she quite enjoyed staying silent and allowing the two Doms to set the scene. Her nipples were tingling, her clit already pulsing in expectation, though her anxiety was genuine. Canes left marks, and that was scary.

"Take off your clothes, Tess," Ryan said at last, turning to her. "We're going to cuff you to the suspension bar while we do the practice session. Being restrained will help put you in the proper submissive headspace while you watch."

Tess kept her eyes on Ryan as she stepped out of her shoes and slipped off her dress. She could feel Mr. Stevenson's intense gaze on her. The cincher was cut low so that the tops of her areolas were visible, and in the thong, her entire ass, save for the narrow line of cloth that covered her crack, was exposed.

She stepped beneath the hanging bar, facing the king-size bed and the window beyond. The two men moved to either side of her.

"Raise your arms," Ryan directed.

As they secured her wrists in the cuffs, her arms were pulled into a taut Y. That delicious, erotic sense of helplessness she always felt when bound settled over her like a warm blanket.

"You look beautiful like that, Tess," Ryan said softly, leaning forward to lightly kiss her lips. "You doing okay, my love?"

"Yes, thank you, Sir," Tess replied, basking in the loving concern that radiated from her Dom.

"She is the very picture of submissive grace," Mr. Stevenson said, admiration in both his tone and his expression.

In spite of her shyness in front of another man, Tess was warmed by his praise.

She watched, at once fascinated and anxious, as Mr. Stevenson took up the cane and demonstrated proper wrist action and arm position on the pillow. After a bit, Ryan took the cane from him and whipped it in the air, letting it land with a thwack against the pillow.

Tess flinched, unable to control her gasp. What had she agreed to? What if she couldn't handle it? A lump rose in her throat that she was unable to swallow away. She closed her eyes and focused on relaxing her breathing, and after a while, she regained control, feeling calmer, though still nervous as hell.

They worked for several more minutes, until Mr. Stevenson said, "You're ready for the real thing, my boy. You're a natural with a cane."

Ryan turned back to Tess, the cane in his hand, a cruel, sexy smile on his handsome face that sent a rush of liquid heat through her body. "How about you, Tess? Are you ready?"

"Yes, Sir," she managed, unable to keep the slight tremble out of her tone.

The two men moved behind her, and she was actually glad she couldn't see their faces, because it meant they couldn't see hers.

She jumped when the cane made its initial contact with her bottom, not because it hurt, but because it startled her. She didn't know who was holding that cane, but it didn't really matter. She was submitting with her body to them both, but with her heart to Ryan.

The cane struck her lightly across both cheeks and continued in a steady manner, the sting slowly intensifying as her skin heated. She began to breathe in rapid, gasping pants.

"Slow your breathing," Ryan urged from behind her. "You're doing really well."

Tess made a conscious effort to comply, and after a few moments, she managed to get more air into her lungs, and her heart eased its erratic pace.

"She's ready for more, I think," Mr. Stevenson said.

"I agree," Ryan replied.

There was a whooshing sound, and then the first crack of real pain as the cane made stinging contact with her flesh. Tess cried out, shocked. But after a moment, the sting edged into something warm, even welcome.

"Beautiful," Ryan breathed, awe evident in his tone.

The cane struck again, another line of fire just below the first. Tess forgot about submissive grace and acceptance as the cane left stripes of white-hot intensity over every inch of her bare bottom. "Ow, ow, ow, ow," she began to chant, squirming and writhing in her restraints, dancing on her toes in a vain effort to avoid the relentless sting. "I can't, I can't…"

"Maybe we should—" Ryan began.

"No," Mr. Stevenson interjected firmly. "This is when you forge ahead. Don't stop too soon. You'll diminish the experience for her. Have faith in her, Ryan. She can take more than you think you can—indeed, more than she thinks she can."

"Yes, you're right," Ryan agreed. "She's very brave."

She could have said her safeword, or even just asked Ryan to stop, and he would have.

But she didn't.

She wanted to keep going, inspired and thrilled by their confidence in her. Though her poor bottom was on fire, so was her cunt, and she had never felt more alive in her life.

The cane continued to whistle and crash against her, but either her skin was adapting to the pain, or something else was at play. The sting was no longer quite as sharp, and something was happening to her that she couldn't seem to control, even if she'd wanted to. Her head had fallen back of its own accord, her lips parting, her breath slowing and deepening along with the rhythm of her heart.

"That's it. That's where you want her, Ryan. There's nothing more exquisite than watching a submissive fly, and being drawn along with her on the journey."

She heard the words, but didn't entirely comprehend what Mr. Stevenson was saying. She was floating somewhere in a peaceful place in the middle of a vast, silent ocean, not quite dreaming, but not quite conscious.

As she drifted, she slowly became aware that the caning had stopped. Mr. Stevenson's voice again penetrated her consciousness. "I'll take my leave now so you can finish the scene in private. The room is paid for through the morning. Please enjoy the champagne, and keep the rig and the cane as small tokens of my appreciation for your sharing your beautiful submissive with me. I do hope we will meet again for another session in the future."

She heard the room door open and then, "Treasure what you have, my dears. Life is so fleeting." The door closed with a soft click.

Her cuffs were released, and she sagged back against Ryan. He lifted her into his arms and then set her gently on her stomach on the bed. "You were perfect," he said as he sat down on the mattress beside her. "The welts are beautiful and you were magnificent."

Somehow, Tess found the strength to lift her head. "What about you, Sir? I want to please you. I want to worship your cock."

Ryan smiled. "We have all night, my love." He put his hand on her head, gently guiding it back to the pillow. She was exhausted, and still caught in the thrall of whatever amazing place the caning had taken her, and she didn't resist.

He drew his fingers lightly over her still very tender bottom, and then slipped his hand between her thighs. She sighed deeply as he stroked her swollen clit and slid a finger inside her. She moaned as he began to move his hand against her cunt, already so aroused that she was almost instantly ready to climax.

"Can I come?" she whispered breathlessly.

"Yes," Ryan replied.

He continued to rub and stroke her as she shuddered in violent orgasm. But, instead of easing his pace until he gently drew his hand away, as was his usual pattern, this time he continued to tease her clit as he thrust his finger in and out of her with perfect friction.

"Please," she panted after a while. "I can't. It's too much. I need to rest." Even as she said this, the wave of a second climax had begun to build inside her.

"I'll tell you when it's time to rest," Ryan said, his tone dominant and sure. "Surrender yourself to me. Give me everything you have."

The wave crashed before she could even ask permission, and she shook with the intensity of the orgasm, which was just as powerful as the first.

Again and again, he pulled the climaxes from her until she was writhing on the bed, panting and gasping, tears streaming down her face. She lost count of the orgasms, becoming pure, raw lust, only dimly aware of where Ryan's hand began and her body ended. Finally, she became aware of a high-pitched keening sound as the last orgasm was wrested from her body.

Then Ryan's arms were around her, and he pulled her into a warm, strong embrace, holding her until her crying gasps and shudders slowly subsided.

"Shh," he whispered as he held her close. "I've got you, baby. You're safe with me. You'll always be safe with me."

Chapter 12

Six months into their relationship, Tess and Ryan formally moved in together. The timing was perfect, as Peter and his girlfriend had gotten engaged, and Peter had moved out of Ryan's place. Though everyone at work knew they were together, no one suspected that the gold chain Tess wore around her neck was in fact a collar from her Dom—a constant, sexy reminder that she was owned in the best possible way by a man who loved her.

Their exercise room now doubled as a BDSM playroom, complete with sturdy hooks in the ceiling that held hanging plants when guests came over, but would support the rope and chain Ryan used to bind her for a whipping or caning, or support the portable leather bondage swing when he wanted to sexually torture her and then fuck her until she was delirious with pleasure.

Though of course they maintained their professional demeanor at work, Ryan would sometimes send a one-word text to Tess—just her name—echoing back to when Mr. Stevenson used to call Olivia into the office with that single word command. When she got the text, if she was able, she was to report to his office.

She would enter silently, locking the door behind her. Before coming any farther into the room, she would remove her panties, which she would then bring to her Master. Ryan would accept them with a sexy smile and not return them until the evening.

Sometimes he would just passionately kiss her, but other times he might swivel his desk chair toward her, revealing his unzipped trousers, his cock already in hand. She had exactly five minutes to make him come, and if she failed, she would be punished when they got home that night. But because the scenario got them both so excited, she never failed to give her lover the satisfaction he demanded. Her reward later that night would be every bit as sexy and thrilling as her punishment would have been.

She would return to her office, sans underwear and on fire with desire, though she was forbidden to touch herself. Sometimes it was very hard to concentrate on her work after those sexy sessions, but she had to admit—she loved every second of it.

When at home, Ryan kept Tess either naked or in one of her growing collections of waist cinchers. She loved the way they made her feel, as if Ryan himself were gripping her waist, laying claim to her. They forced her to move with a certain grace, and she'd taken to wearing them at work too, hidden beneath her conservative suits.

Tess had never been happier, and the delicious irony of being Ryan's submissive at home was not lost on her. The confidence and joy she gained from achieving submissive grace was mirrored back in her professional life. She attacked each workday with vigor and energy, and her latest performance review had been glowingly positive, and accompanied by a very nice raise.

They continued to meet with Mr. Stevenson from time to time, sometimes for a scene, sometimes just for a meal. He had brought a friend to their last dinner, a woman named Lorraine Pickford, whom he'd met on a BDSM singles site. "My grandchildren gave me a laptop for my ninety-third birthday," Mr. Stevenson explained. "They were very patient showing me how to do email and use this internet thing. I had no *idea* what all was out there," he'd added with a decidedly mischievous gleam in his eye as he patted Lorraine's hand.

Though in her eighties, Lorraine was still beautiful, with dark, intelligent eyes, high cheekbones and a generous mouth. Tess found the way they held hands and kept smiling at each other and exchanging secret looks very touching. "Lorraine's new to the scene," Mr. Stevenson explained, "but one day I hope she'll be ready to allow you both to witness her submissive grace, just as the two of you have honored me."

One evening when Ryan and Tess came home after a long workday, a small box with Tess's name on it was waiting by the front door. She didn't recognize the return address. "Huh," she said. "I don't remember ordering anything. I wonder what it is."

"I guess you'll just have to open it and see," Ryan said, attempting a deadpan expression though his dancing eyes gave him away.

Tess sat on the sofa in the living room and opened the box. She took out a small cloth pouch. Inside was a pair of what she guessed were nipple clamps, though they were different from the alligator clip type Ryan sometimes used on her. She pressed the sides of one of the oval metal rings to open the rubber-tipped clamps.

"Ouch, these look dangerous," she said with a shiver.

Ryan's smile was at once sexy and cruel. "Not dangerous, but definitely not for beginners. They're called clover clamps." He sat beside her. "There should be another pair in there."

Tess reached into the bubble wrap and found another pouch. Ryan took it from her and drew out a second set of clamps. He pushed open the spring mechanism. "The cool thing about these beauties is when you pull on them, instead of popping off, they actually get tighter." He let it snap shut.

Tess dropped the clamps, her hands flying involuntarily to her breasts to cover her nipples. "You think I can handle that?"

"I know you can, my love." Ryan stroked her thigh, pushing her skirt up and moving his hand slowly toward her bare pussy, as she'd given her panties to him that afternoon in his office.

"Spread your legs," he directed.

As Tess shifted to obey, her mind suddenly focused in on the second set of clamps. She sat up, abruptly slamming her legs closed. "Whoa. Wait a minute. What's the second set of clamps for?" she asked, afraid of the answer.

Ryan pushed her gently back against the cushions and slid his hand under her skirt, forcing her to part her thighs. He cupped her cunt and rubbed his palm against her clit. "What do you think they're for, sub girl?"

Tess moaned as he stroked and teased her as only he knew how. "Ryan, I couldn't. It would hurt too much."

"You can do what I tell you to do, Tess. Surely you know that by now? You trust me, right? I wouldn't give you more than you can handle."

Despite her trepidation, her clit was throbbing beneath his touch, her sex swelling and opening like a flower. Still, she couldn't help but shudder at the thought of those hard, unyielding clamps gripping her delicate labia.

Correctly reading her fear, Ryan took her into his arms. "Remember, you're courageous and strong. This is just another step on our D/s journey, another chance for you to show your submissive grace."

"Yes, Sir. Thank you for reminding me."

"You're welcome, my love. Now, stand up and take off your

clothes. I want to clamp your nipples and your lovely cunt."

When she was naked, Ryan stood and stepped behind her. As he nuzzled her neck with kisses, he brought his hand to her throat and wrapped his fingers around it, sending a tremor of submissive desire through her entire body.

"Who do you belong to?" he whispered into her ear.

"You, Sir," she murmured back, trying to twist around to kiss him. But he held her still, increasing the pressure at her throat so that she gasped, her heart thudding in her chest.

After a moment, he let her go and turned her to face him, staring down at her with those sea glass green eyes. "Tonight you will prove it once again. Hold up your breasts in offering."

Tess obeyed, her eyes on her lover as he picked up a pair of clamps.

He gripped her left nipple between his thumb and index finger, pulling it taut. With his other hand, he opened one of the clamps, positioned it over her nipple and let the spring close.

"Ow," Tess cried, jerking back herself. "That really hurts."

"But it's nothing you can't handle, brave girl," Ryan assured her, his eyes gleaming with sadistic lust. "Now stand still so I can clamp the other one."

Tess forced herself back into position, her heart hammering against her ribs. In spite of the pain, or no, precisely because of it, her cunt ached with need as she waited with trepidation for the second fierce pinch.

As it closed over her right nipple, Tess managed to remain still, expressing her pain in a long hiss of breath through pursed lips. The short silver chain that held the clamps together swayed against her breasts. She was already ascending to that dark, perfect place in her psyche where pleasure and pain lost separate meaning, and all she wanted to do was please her Master.

Ryan guided her gently back down to the couch. He crouched in front of her with the second wicked pair.

Tess closed her eyes as Ryan parted her thighs and stroked her pussy with sure fingers. "You were born to suffer for me, isn't that right, sub girl?" His voice was low and husky with desire.

"Yes, Sir."

She drew in a breath as he tugged gently at her right outer labia and positioned the clamp on either side. He released the mechanism and it clamped her like a vise.

"Fuck," she whispered.

"Shh," Ryan soothed. "You're doing great." He pulled at the left labia and closed the clamp on her tender flesh. "Slow your breathing. Focus on how much you're pleasing me right now."

She was whimpering softly, but somehow managed to take a deep breath, which she let out slowly.

"Better, yes? The pain should be easing now—your nerve endings growing numb."

He was right. While the clamps on her nipples and labia still hurt, the pain was tolerable, and the erotic overlay of dark desire was undeniable.

Ryan leaned closer, his hands resting on her spread thighs. His tongue snaked out, licking against her throbbing clit.

She groaned with pleasure, which wrapped like a ribbon around the erotic pain.

He licked and kissed her until she was panting, a climax building inside her. When he slid one finger and then two inside her, she screamed with pleasure and cried out, "Please, Sir. Can I come?"

"Yes."

He added another finger, moving it like a cock inside her as he licked her to a powerful orgasm that left her nearly unconscious with its power. She was only dimly aware when he lifted her into his arms, but then she snuggled against his chest as he carried her through the house and into the bedroom.

He laid her gently on the bed and quickly stripped out of his clothes. Sitting beside her, he said, "I'm going to take them off now, Tess. It's going to hurt, but only for a second or two."

He removed the labia clamps first, and Tess flinched as the blood rushed back, reawakening her tortured nerve endings. The nipples were worse, and she cried out at the stinging pain, though, as promised, it only lasted a few seconds before subsiding into a dull but not unpleasant ache.

Ryan draped himself over her, and she wrapped her arms and legs eagerly around him, welcoming his heavy masculine body over hers, and the press of his hard cock between her legs. "You're perfect," he whispered ardently as he entered her wetness. "And you're mine."

A few weeks after the introduction of the clover clamps, Ryan brought up the idea of labial piercing, showing her a few pictures online that, Tess had to admit, looked pretty sexy. Nevertheless, she had categorically refused to consider piercing for herself. No way in hell was someone going to put a needle through her labia. Just the thought made her cringe.

He hadn't pressed her, and they'd dropped the subject. But Tess hadn't forgotten. She began to do some research online about body piercing. She couldn't help but admire the beautiful jewelry some of the women wore in their piercings, and though her mind continued to rebel, her body responded to the images—her nipples hardening, her cunt moistening.

She recalled the scene in *Charlotte's Awakening*, which had both fascinated and horrified her when she'd first read it. Thumbing through the well-worn novel, she found the passage again.

"It's not enough to mark you with the whip. It's not enough that you wear my chains at your throat, your wrists, your ankles. I want you to wear my chains at your sex. Indeed, I command it."

Charlotte kept her head down, eyes downcast as she had been taught by her Master. She was still as a statue, the only evidence that she had even heard him a slight movement of her bare shoulders.

Sir Jonathan pulled her up by the arm and stared into her eyes. "I want it to be permanent, Charlotte. I'm going to pierce your flesh and lock your sex with these chains." He held up a bracelet of fine gold. One end of the clasp came to a very sharp point. The other end was a spring mechanism that, once engaged, would not open again.

As Charlotte paled, Sir Jonathan went on, "Tonight when I come for you, I will find you naked in the bath. This piercing is yet another proof that you belong completely and utterly to me."

He caught her as she swayed and fainted into his arms. Her display, while charming, would gain her no pity and certainly no reprieve.

Tess shivered even though she knew the words were fiction. She was glad Ryan never "informed her" of what she "would do." While she adored submitting to her dominant lover, the exchange of power was always and completely voluntary.

But as the weeks passed, Tess couldn't stop thinking about the piercing. Her research led her to understand it wasn't as painful as a nipple piercing, as there were fewer nerve endings in the labia. The process was quick and the result was undeniably sexy. And if the jewelry didn't work, she could always take it out. There would be no permanent spring mechanisms for her, thank you very much.

One night after dinner about a month after his initial broaching of the topic, the two of them sat at the table, sharing a glass of merlot. "I think I want to do it," Tess blurted suddenly, clenching her hands into fists of resolve. "I think maybe I'm ready."

Ryan looked at her. "Want to do what? Ready for what?"

"The piercing. I love the symbolism of it—another act of submission that only you and I would know about." She touched the gold chain around her throat. "Like this secret collar, except even sexier."

Ryan set down his wineglass and regarded her with a bemused smile. "I thought that one was a hard limit no-go. I didn't even know you were still considering it."

"Well," Tess replied, heat moving over her face. "I have been. And I-I…" The import of what she was saying suddenly made her dizzy. But she forged on. "I think I want it."

He chuckled and shook his head. "That's not exactly a ringing declaration, Tess. We'll revisit the subject in the future, when you're more sure."

"But I—"

He leaned over and kissed her forehead. "It's okay, my love. Truly. I love that you're thinking about it, but you're not ready."

Tess snapped her mouth closed and glared at Ryan. How dare he take the wind out of her sails like that? Here she had geared herself up to do this supremely submissive act, and he was telling her no. What the hell?

But then she took a step back, replaying how she'd presented herself. *I think maybe…* Ryan was right. She wasn't ready. Yet.

"Okay," she said softly. "Okay."

Four more days passed, and while neither of them brought up the subject of her piercing, it was never far from Tess's thoughts. Though it was Saturday morning, Ryan had to work, and Tess decided to do a little shopping. She went to a body piercing shop called Rings of Desire, which she'd determined from online reviews was the best around.

She perused the body jewelry for a while, and then noticed a framed photograph on the wall that at first she thought was a close-up of a butterfly wearing jewelry. As she examined it, she saw it was actually a woman's shaved, spread pussy, tattooed to look like butterfly wings, the bulk of the design on the mons above the cleft. The inner labia were its lower wings, and they and the clit hood were decorated with numerous rings. The effect was stunning, if a little frightening, and Tess couldn't stop staring at the picture.

"You like it?"

"It's amazing," Tess admitted, turning to a tall, statuesque woman with rings in her eyebrows and nose, along with multiple piercings along each ear.

"Thanks. My boyfriend did the tattoo art, I did the piercings. My name is Sandra and this is my shop. Can I help you find something today?"

"I'm thinking," Tess began, but then stopped herself. No more equivocating. "I want to get my labia pierced," she said firmly. "I'm looking for the right piece of jewelry."

"You came to the right place on both counts. Let me show you what we've got."

There was so much to choose from. Eventually, Tess selected a small gold hoop shaped like a horseshoe, with ruby posts on either end.

"They're removable, see?" Sandra said, unscrewing one of the posts to demonstrate. "You can take it off, just like earrings."

"And the piercing," Tess asked, swallowing her fear. "The needle...?"

"Honey, it's a piece of cake," Sandra said with a smile. "One-two-three and done, and you'll be so happy with it, I promise."

When Ryan came home from the office that afternoon, Tess was waiting for him at the front door, naked and on her knees. She held out the jewelry box on her palms.

"What's this?" Ryan set down his briefcase and took the box from her hands. He opened it and examined the small gold and ruby piece. "Is this what I think it is?" The play of emotions on his face was part admiration, part concern and all love. "Are you saying you're ready, Tess?" he asked softly. "That you definitively want this?"

Tess rose to her feet and looked her darling Master in the eye. "Yes," she replied in a calm, determined voice. "I'm ready, Sir. I want to be pierced."

Tess leaned back on the comfortable recliner in the back room of Sandra's shop, naked from the waist down, covered with a paper blanket like they used at doctors' offices. The space was clean and bright, and Ryan sat beside her on a stool, holding her hand.

Sandra swabbed the area Tess and Ryan had selected for the piercing and used a plastic clamp to hold the skin taut. "This way you only pierce the minimum amount of tissue, resulting in the minimum amount of pain," she explained. She dabbed some gel on the spot. "This will numb you up nicely so you'll hardly feel a thing."

Tess looked away as Sandra unwrapped a fresh piercing needle, and Ryan gave her hand a steadying squeeze.

"Okay," Sandra said. "Close your eyes and relax. I'm going to count to three and you just take nice, deep breaths." She stroked Tess's hair, her touch soothing. On the count of three, she slipped the needle through the delicate labial fold. Tess felt a pinch, but nothing she couldn't easily tolerate.

Though Tess kept her eyes averted, she knew from her research that, once the piercing needle was withdrawn, it left a hollow plastic catheter still sticking through the skin. Sandra would insert the stem of the ring into the catheter and then remove the plastic, leaving the jewelry in place. She would then screw the gem post onto the stud and that would be that.

"All done," Sandra announced. "Told you. Piece of cake."

Tess opened her eyes. "Wow," she said. "That was quick."

"Want to see?" Sandra brought over a hand mirror and handed it to Tess.

"Oh, I love it," Tess cried, thrilled.

She turned to Ryan, who was smiling at her, love light spilling from his eyes. "I love it, too," he said. "I love you."

It was one year to the day since their first date and, as Tess luxuriated in the bath, she stared down at the sparkling emerald-cut diamond ring on her finger, which was flanked by lovely blue sapphires. When Ryan had asked her to marry him, she had joyously accepted.

She slipped a hand between her legs, fingering the golden and ruby jewel tucked into the folds of her pussy. She stroked herself, though she wouldn't make herself come. She was never to masturbate without Ryan's express permission. Rather than feeling restricted by this command, she thrilled to it, as she did all of their BDSM rules and rituals.

Tess thought with a wistful sigh about Olivia's secret diary, and how it had helped Ryan and her begin their own D/s journey, which was now so central to their relationship. While Tess knew from the journals and from Mr. Stevenson that their affair had been fulfilling, it must have been hard and lonely for Olivia not to have been able to share her true sexual nature with her husband. Tess was grateful her lover was also her partner and soon-to-be husband.

She soaked a while longer in the fragrant water, and then climbed out to dry herself. She was surprised to see Ryan lying on the bed when she came out of the bathroom, as he had been ensconced in the study pouring over a legal brief when she'd gone to bathe.

He was naked, his cock fisted in his hand. He smiled a lazy, seductive smile. "Come here, sexy girl," he commanded.

Tess dropped her towel and joined him on the bed, reveling in his strong arms as they wrapped around her.

Ryan drew a finger down her cheek, moving it over her lips so they parted. She sucked on the finger and he slid it deep into her mouth, like a cock. As she gave herself over to her Master, Tess slipped effortlessly into that wonderful submissive state of utter peace intertwined with fiery passion. It was a delicious and potent dichotomy that never lost its power.

After a while, Ryan pulled his finger away and looked at Tess, the love in his eyes so bright she actually caught her breath.

"I belong to you," she whispered, her heart bursting with love.

"We belong to each other," he answered. Then he took her once more into his arms.

Check out all Claire's books at https://clairethompson.net